KIDNAPPED IN LITTLE LEAF CREEK

LITTLE LEAF CREEK COZY MYSTERIES
BOOK TWENTY-SIX

CINDY BELL

Copyright © 2025 Cindy Bell

All rights reserved.

Cover Design by Lou Harper, Cover Affairs

All rights reserved. No part of this publication may be reproduced or transmitted in any form or by any means, electronic or mechanical, including photocopy, recording, or any information storage or retrieval system, without permission in writing from the publisher.

This is a work of fiction. The characters, incidents and locations portrayed in this book and the names herein are fictitious. Any similarity to or identification with the locations, names, characters or history of any person, product or entity is entirely coincidental and unintentional.

All trademarks and brands referred to in this book are for illustrative purposes only, are the property of their respective owners and not affiliated with this publication in any way. Any trademarks are being used without permission, and the publication of the trademark is not authorized by, associated with or sponsored by the trademark owner.

ISBN: 9798313704814

CHAPTER 1

Cassie Alberta-Vail rolled over in bed and groaned as she heard yet another series of panicked barks. They were muffled enough that she knew they weren't coming from inside her house, but clear enough that she recognized them right away. They belonged to her neighbor Tessa Watters' collie mix, Harry. But he never barked before sunrise. She started to pull her pillow over her head to block out the sound, but a sudden sense of urgency outweighed the annoyance at being woken. She bolted out of bed.

"Cassie?" Sebastian Vail, Cassie's husband, mumbled from beside her and reached out in an attempt to pull her close. "What's wrong?"

"It's probably nothing. Just go back to sleep." Cassie quickly threw a light robe over her pajamas, slipped on some shoes, grabbed her cell phone from the bedside table, and ran for the front door.

As Cassie rushed down the steps of her front porch and sprinted toward Tessa's house, her mind wandered, worried that her best friend was sick, injured, or worse. With Tessa being in her seventies, it did cross Cassie's mind that health issues could be a concern, but the independent woman prided herself on being fit as a fiddle. Cassie clung to that fact as she tried to remain calm.

She opened the gate that led from her driveway into Tessa's yard and found two lively goats and one barking dog, all very active before the sun had even started rising. The goats, Gerry and Billy, seemed absolutely gleeful at the dog's wild behavior.

"Harry, what is it?" Cassie glanced at him while still making her way toward Tessa's front porch.

"Can you believe it?" Tessa's voice carried from the front door. "I just can't get him to calm down."

A wave of relief carried through Cassie as she heard, then saw, her friend. She appeared to be in one piece and not experiencing any kind of medical emergency.

"I was so worried something was wrong." Cassie pressed her hand against her chest.

"I put Harry outside because he was barking so much. I thought he would calm down if I let him loose, but it's not working. Now he just wants out of the yard so bad. I've tried giving him treats. At this point my only option is to load him up in the jeep and take him for a drive. Otherwise, he's going to wake up the whole neighborhood." Tessa turned back toward the house. "Let me grab his leash."

As Tessa stepped back inside her house, Cassie walked toward Harry who had the goats chasing after him as he ran the perimeter of the fence, searching for a way out.

"Harry, it's okay, boy. Whatever it is, we can figure it out." Cassie patted her knee in an attempt to summon him toward her. Usually, he was very friendly and eager to greet her, but today he seemed focused on only one goal.

Harry ignored Cassie as he rounded up the goats, gathering them close to the fence line.

The goats lined up against the fence, then one hopped onto the other. Within a split second, Harry launched from one goat to the next, then sailed right over the fence into the field of the farm that backed up to their houses. The farm that Sebastian owned and ran, and his sister, Stephanie Vail, currently lived on.

"Oh no! Harry, get back here!" Cassie gasped as Tessa stepped back outside with his leash in her hand. "Tessa, he's escaped! I'm calling Stephanie, now. He's on Sebastian's farm."

"Let's go. Maybe we can catch him before he gets off the property. There's no use trying to run after him in the dark." Tessa hurried for the jeep. "He must really be rattled by something." She turned on the engine while Cassie hopped into the passenger seat.

As Cassie and Tessa drove along the road bordering the farm, Cassie scanned the vegetable fields for any sign of the dog. Her heart skipped a beat when, for just a second, a flash of silver and white appeared above the treetops.

"What is that?" Cassie's mind raced in an attempt to understand what she saw.

"What did you see?"

"I don't know. I honestly don't know. There's a break in the fence just there. Let me out, so I can get a closer look." Cassie pointed to the fence line ahead of them.

Tessa slowed the jeep to a stop. "You know, with

my leg, I won't be able to keep up with him." She'd been shot while on duty as a police officer.

"Don't worry. You drive, I'll run. I can get closer on foot." Cassie felt the full force of her forty-plus years creep into her muscles, but she ignored it as she ran alongside the field and searched for any hint of the collie mix.

A few seconds later, the silver flash she'd seen suddenly emerged from the field and ran right out in front of her.

"Is that a horse?" Cassie chased after it at first, but its large size and loud movements startled her. She froze for a moment as she watched a large stallion, whose coat looked almost silver, gallop in the opposite direction. Was she dreaming?

"Cassie! Get back in here!" The jeep stopped beside her as Tessa waved for her to get in.

Cassie climbed in, out of breath from chasing after the dog, who she saw bolt after the horse.

"We're going to need some backup. Ollie has to get some squad cars out here to help out." Tessa continued after Harry and the horse. "I'll keep up with them. You let him know what's going on."

Cassie pulled out her phone and dialed Detective Oliver Graham's number and put it on speaker.

"Ollie, you're not going to believe this. We have a horse on the loose. It's running on the side of the road, along the farms." Cassie rattled off their current location. "Can you get some lights and sirens out here to help?"

"Sure, I can do that. A horse, you said?" Oliver's voice was still sleepy. "That's a new one. What a way to start the day."

"Harry's after him!" Tessa called out. "He won't listen to me. He won't stop chasing him."

Oliver's tone quickly filled with concern. "I'll be right there."

Cassie ended the call as her heart continued to pound both from running and the urge to make sure both animals were safe.

"It looks like someone's already joined us." Tessa looked through the rearview mirror at a motorcycle that followed along behind them.

Cassie looked over her shoulder and peered through the early morning sunlight that was peeking out. "That's Stephanie. She must have decided to join in to help."

"There's a couple of ranches ahead." Tessa knew the area well.

In the distance, sirens shrieked through the otherwise quiet morning air.

"Ollie's not far behind us, either." Cassie breathed a sigh of relief. "With this much help, I'm sure we'll get them corralled in no time."

"Well, it sure looks like the horse knows where it belongs." Tessa squinted through the windshield as the horse turned down the long dirt road of a ranch. "I wonder if anyone's noticed he's missing. Let's go make sure he gets home and give Harry a serious talking-to."

Cassie watched the horse run. She didn't have much experience with horses, but something about his movements made her uneasy.

"Tessa, isn't it odd that he'd be all the way in town but he's heading back toward the ranches? And why do you think he ran in the first place?"

"I'm not sure. Maybe he just had a strange urge." Tessa parked beside three other vehicles. A pickup truck, a sedan, and an SUV. "I think that someone must be home, with all these cars here. Now, where did the animals go?" she huffed as she stepped out of the jeep. "They were just here."

"There, Tessa." Cassie pointed toward a flash of silver just as Stephanie, followed closely by Oliver, pulled into the driveway behind them.

Oliver shut off his flashing lights and stepped out of his car.

Stephanie pulled off her helmet as she bolted toward them, breathless. "Did you catch Harry?"

"He followed a horse into that barn." Cassie had already begun walking toward it, when the horse inside let out a loud, long neigh.

CHAPTER 2

"Wait here. I'll go check it out. The horse might be spooked." Oliver walked toward the barn doors.

"And what about you?" Tessa trailed after him. A motherly tone entered her voice. "When have you ever had anything to do with a horse?"

"Tessa, there are some things you don't know about me." Oliver shot her a stern look. "Now, stay here. I'll be right out with Harry." He continued on into the barn.

"It's okay. We'll be right here if Ollie needs our help." Cassie stepped closer to Tessa, worried she might just take off into the barn.

"I do know something about horses, and he's right." Stephanie moved over to join them. "A spooked horse can be very dangerous. If Sebastian was here he could help. He's great with horses. Where is he?" She met Cassie's eyes.

"Oh, I told him to go back to sleep." Cassie winced. "He's going to be annoyed that he missed all of this."

"Yes, that's probably true." Stephanie continued to watch the doors of the barn as random neighs and whinnies carried out through them. "But it's probably for the best. Ollie might not have let him in there anyway, and you know how those two get sometimes."

"I do," Cassie said.

When Cassie first moved to town, she'd gone on a disastrous date with Oliver, only to soon find herself in love with Sebastian. Time had passed, she and Sebastian had gotten married, and Oliver had gained his own little family when he fell for Cassie's boss, Mirabel Light, who was the guardian of a young teen, Maisy. Yet, tension between the two men still ran thick on occasion. It had less to do with Cassie, and more to do with their personalities clashing.

"Tessa, maybe we should knock on the door and see if anyone's home. They'll want to know that the horse got out." Cassie looked up at the large house.

She hoped that distracting her would give Oliver a little more time to settle down the horse.

"If they haven't come out, with this commotion, then they probably won't wake up to a knock on the door." Tessa relaxed her fists and wrung her hands instead. "Let's see what comes of this, first. I don't know exactly what's happened here, but I know I have a bad feeling about it." She scanned the horizon, the house, then the road that led to the driveway, before looking back at the barn. "I can't quite place it, but I can't shake it, either."

Cassie had to resist the urge to burst through the barn doors. She could hear scuffling, as well as a few muffled grumbles as she presumed Oliver was attempting to wrangle the horse. The horse had caused a lot of chaos, but she had to admit, she'd never seen a more beautiful horse.

"It's quieter now," Stephanie whispered to Tessa and Cassie. "He must have gotten control of the horse."

"Harry's not barking anymore, either." Concern etched Tessa's normally indifferent expression. All the toughness she carried after years of working as a police officer seemed to vanish as she worried about her beloved dog.

"I'm sure Ollie will bring him out in just a

second." Cassie tried to fill her voice with confidence.

She realized that she should tell Sebastian what was happening. One thing they'd been working on in their still young marriage was communication. She'd promised to be better at keeping him up to date on things, and he'd promised to be better at letting her know when he was feeling disconnected or concerned about her distance.

She'd spent years married to a man who couldn't care less what she did or where she was. He'd married her in her early twenties, and she'd moved into his expensive penthouse as a model wife. Adjusting to being with a man who had a genuine interest in her was both invigorating and an uphill battle with her own ingrained habits.

Sebastian was starting work a bit later today, but he would be up now, ready to head to the farm. As Cassie began typing out a text to him to update him on the situation, she wished he were at her side. She knew he would make everyone feel calmer. He had the kindest heart and an unshakable patience that left her absolutely impressed, especially since she could be a little fiery at times. Straight after she sent the text, she heard Oliver's heavy steps approach the barn doors.

"Stay back." Oliver stepped out and used the full width of his broad shoulders and arms to block the entrance to the barn. Although this still left some space around him, his commanding presence filled up the rest. "No one's allowed inside. This is a crime scene."

"Harry!" Tessa crouched down and slapped her knees. "Harry, you come out here right now!"

Harry bolted out of the barn and around Oliver, straight into Tessa's arms. She cradled the dog close.

Cassie's heartbeat quickened as she noticed tears in Tessa's eyes. Tessa presented herself as a very stern woman without a lot of room for emotion, except when it came to her pets.

Oliver spoke softly to an officer who'd just arrived. He turned back toward them with a grave expression.

"What do you mean it's a crime scene, Ollie? What happened in there?" Cassie asked.

Before Oliver could answer, a man stepped out onto the porch of the large ranch-style house that sprawled across the width of the driveway. He made his way down the steps.

"What's going on out here? Why are all of you people on my property? Detective, why are you here?" The man scowled as he tried to peer past

Oliver. "Where's Lisbeth? Lisbeth? Lisbeth are you in there?"

"Richard, you're going to need to take a step back." Oliver stretched his arm out to block Richard's attempts to get through the door.

"What are you talking about? This is my property. This is my barn. My sister should be in there." Richard's voice raised.

Cassie covered her mouth to muffle a gasp as she realized Lisbeth must be dead, and Oliver was shielding Richard from seeing her. If she were only injured, Oliver would be in the barn trying to help her. He would have called an ambulance, and it would have arrived by now. But there was no sign of one. And Oliver's expression hadn't gotten any softer.

Cassie's mind spun. Had Lisbeth had a terrible accident? But that wouldn't make it a crime scene, would it?

"Richard, I need you to calm down, please." Oliver glanced over at Tessa who'd hooked the leash on to Harry's collar.

She passed the leash over to Cassie, then gave Oliver a short nod as she stepped forward to shield the other side of the entrance to the barn.

"Richard." Tessa locked eyes with him as her

voice took on a steady but empathetic tone. "You can't go inside right now. This barn's a crime scene."

"What?" Richard stumbled back a few steps.

Stephanie stepped up beside Cassie and slipped her arm through hers.

"I'm sorry to have to tell you this, Richard." Oliver cleared his throat. "Lisbeth is dead. It looks like she was killed."

Richard's face froze with his mouth hanging wide open. His legs wobbled and he staggered back a step. Stephanie and Cassie moved to either side of him and placed their hands on his arms to steady him.

Cassie's thoughts swirled in shock as Oliver's words echoed in her mind. Lisbeth wasn't just dead. She'd been murdered!

CHAPTER 3

"We're right here with you." Cassie kept a hand on Richard's arm.

"Are you sure?" Richard looked at Oliver through tear-filled eyes. "Are you sure it's Lisbeth? Is she really gone?"

"Yes, I'm sure. I'm sorry for your loss." Oliver took a step toward him. "From what I can tell, she died within the last hour or two."

"Oh, Lisbeth!" Richard cried out. "Why? Why her? She didn't deserve this!"

Cassie continued to hold her hand on his arm as her stomach tied into knots.

"I know this is a huge shock." Oliver looked straight into Richard's eyes. "But I need you to help me figure out who did this to your sister. So, I need you to focus. Can you do that?"

"Oh, Lisbeth!" Richard wiped his hand across his face. "How can I help you figure out anything? It makes no sense to me! No one would want to hurt her! Everyone loves her!"

"You seemed to know that your sister was in the barn." Cassie scrutinized his expression. Despite his display of grief, it appeared as if he was the only other person there. "Why was that? Did she tell you she'd be there?"

"That's where she always is. That's Lisbeth." Richard clasped his hands together. "I mean, she takes care of the horses, and feeds them in the morning. And when I get up, she's always in the barn or just leaving it."

"So, she's normally an early riser?" Oliver pulled a notebook and pen out of his pocket. "When was the last time you saw her?"

"I don't know." Richard sighed. "Maybe, I guess, around dinnertime last night."

"You had dinner together?" Oliver started to make a note.

"No, that's just the last time that I saw her. She was coming home, I was finishing up my glass of wine, and we exchanged a few words before she went to her room." Richard took a shaky breath. "If I'd known it was going to be the last time I would see her alive, I obviously would have had a lot more to say."

"So, after she went to her room you didn't see her again? Or hear her?" Oliver asked.

"No, I went to my room. It's clear on the other side of the house." Richard pointed in that direction. "I took a few sleeping pills, and I went to bed." He ran his hand back through his hair. "I just can't believe this."

An officer grabbed a wooden chair from beside the porch and carried it over to Richard. He gestured for him to sit in it.

Richard sank down onto the chair.

"Richard, who else lives with you in the house? Is there anyone visiting?" Oliver kept his gaze focused on him.

"No one's visiting, no. But Drake, our younger brother, he lives here with us. And Chase, the ranch hand, he lives in a trailer on the property." Richard pointed in another direction. "He should be here. He should have been working with Lisbeth," he muttered as he pulled his phone out of his pocket. "I need to tell my brother."

"Do you know where he is?" Oliver looked toward the quiet house, then back to him.

"No. He's usually still sleeping, but occasionally he goes for an early morning walk around the property. His door was open, and he wasn't in his room when I came out here, so he's probably walking somewhere on the ranch. I'll call him." Richard tapped on his phone. "Why are you asking me so many questions about Drake?"

"I'm trying to piece together what happened." Oliver's voice remained even. "I'm trying to get as much information as I can about what Lisbeth did before her death. She might have been with Drake, or he might know something."

"There's no answer," Richard said.

"I need to speak to him as soon as possible. Do you have any idea where he might be? Or any other numbers I could reach him at?" Oliver asked.

"Ollie." Cassie looked toward the bush not far from the barn, as she heard a strange sound. "I think I hear a buzzing coming from that bush."

"Cassie, I don't have time to talk about bees right now." Oliver shot a brief scowl in her direction before looking back at Richard. "Try calling him again, please."

"Okay, fine, but he's not answering. He does

that sometimes when he doesn't want to deal with me." Richard rolled his eyes, then dialed the number again.

Cassie walked over to the bush and listened. The buzzing she heard suddenly became more distinct and recognizable. "Ollie!" She spun around to look at him just as he shot her an exasperated look. "I think it's a phone." She dug through the bush until she felt something solid under her fingertips. She closed her hand around it and pulled it out of the bush. "It is a phone."

All eyes swung to the device in her hand. After a moment, Richard took a step forward.

"That's Drake's phone. I'd recognize that green cover anywhere." Richard stared at it with wide eyes. "No wonder he's not answering it." He peered at the bush. "But what would it be doing in there? He's always so careful with his phone. He never lets it out of his sight."

"Let me see it, Cassie." Oliver walked over to her with his gloved hand out.

"Wait, just a second." Richard rushed to move between them. "You can't just take someone's phone. It doesn't belong to you."

"I'm just having a look." Oliver continued to hold out his hand to Cassie.

Cassie sensed the tension between the two men. She knew she had to follow Oliver's instructions. She dropped the phone into his hand before Richard could grab it from hers.

"Give that here!" Richard took a step toward Oliver.

"Easy, Richard." Tessa touched his arm and guided him away from Oliver who was now in a defensive stance. "We all want the same thing here, don't we? Oliver isn't going to do anything he shouldn't do with that phone."

"I'm sorry, I'm sorry," Richard mumbled as he stepped back from her. "All of this is just such a shock, and I don't know what's right and what's wrong. Drake would. Where is he?" He stared at the barn. "He's not in there, too, is he?"

"No, no one else is in there. I did a full search. There are only horses inside. I have an officer with them." Oliver looked over the phone. "It doesn't look damaged. Can you give me Chase's number, please?"

Richard checked his phone and rattled off the number.

Oliver pulled out his own phone and called Chase. After a few seconds he left a message for Chase to call him. "No answer. It goes to voicemail."

He ended the call and looked up at Richard. "We came here because a horse was on the loose. Do you know how the horse escaped?"

"No idea." Richard covered his face with his hands. "I just can't believe this. How could this happen? I need to see her. I need to see Lisbeth."

"Not yet, sorry." Oliver frowned. "Right now, the best thing we can do is work together. We need to figure out what happened to your sister, and where your brother and Chase are. I'll have someone check Chase's trailer."

CHAPTER 4

*assie's curiosity kicked into overdrive. She had a million questions, and felt as if some of the answers were just inside the barn. At the moment, one was the most prominent. Who killed Lisbeth?

Oliver spoke into the phone and turned toward his officers. "We have a possible suspect on the loose."

"Suspect?" Richard glared at him. "You aren't talking about Drake, are you?"

"We have to explore all avenues. If he left his phone behind, that's a good indication that he ran." Oliver barked a few orders into his radio before holstering it again. "Officers all over the county will be searching for Drake. Until he's been found, and

I've spoken to him, I consider him a person of interest. So, if you hear from him, you need to tell me." His tone sharpened. "Richard? Are you listening to me? If you hear from him, you absolutely have to tell me."

"I will. I hope he's okay. What if he's hurt?" Richard's dazed expression gave way to fear as he looked toward the red pickup truck. "That's his truck. And his phone's here. He wouldn't go anywhere without either."

"He might if he was on the run. My officers will search the house and the rest of the property for him." Oliver turned away from Richard to speak to a couple of officers who'd just arrived.

"I can't believe this." Richard stared at the barn.

"Richard, can I get your number?" Cassie asked. "I would like it so I can check in on you."

"Sure." Richard gave her his number, and she jotted it down in her notebook.

"And here's mine." Cassie tore out a slip of paper and handed it to him. "Call me if you need anything, okay? This has been a huge shock."

"Thank you." Richard took the paper and entered the number into his phone.

An officer approached to question him further

and take him to search the house to see if there was any sign of Drake inside.

Cassie took a few steps back to try to make sense of her own thoughts. She heard Stephanie and Tessa chatting, but didn't follow the conversation. She didn't want to believe that Drake could kill his sister.

Oliver walked back over to them. "Listen, I think it's best if you all clear out. We have a lot to sort through. One of my officers just checked. Chase isn't in his trailer, so we have two people we have to find. As soon as I know anything, I'll let you know. All right?" He looked at each of them in turn.

Cassie wanted to protest. She wanted to insist that Richard should have someone with him at a time like this. But she knew Oliver had it covered.

Tessa agreed, with a slight nod. "Yes, it's best if you sort it out." She looked over at Stephanie. "Are you okay to get home? If not, you can ride with us. We can drop you off."

"No, it's okay. I'm okay." Stephanie looked at the barn one last time. "It's just hard to believe."

"Yes, it is." Tessa stared at the barn as well before walking off toward the jeep with Harry.

Cassie followed after them and climbed into the passenger side. She sent Sebastian a quick text explaining that she was on the road and heading back home.

Tessa pulled the door to the jeep shut, then looked over at Cassie with wide eyes. "Well, that morning escalated quickly."

"Yes, it did. I'm still trying to make sense of it."

"You and me both." Tessa stared out through the windshield at the cordoned-off barn, then turned the key in the ignition. "I guess Harry must have smelled the horse in the field, or sensed him somehow."

"Maybe he heard him." Cassie chewed on her bottom lip as Tessa drove down the driveway. "I have a theory, but you might think I'm crazy."

"It wouldn't be the first time." Tessa offered a faint smile. "And it probably won't be the last."

"Gee, thanks." Cassie rolled her eyes but smiled. "How do you think the horse got out?"

"Maybe it escaped during the commotion? Maybe the killer let the horse loose? Maybe they hoped it would be a distraction?" Tessa turned out onto the main road. "But that doesn't tell me your theory."

"What if the horse escaped to look for help?" Cassie winced as she looked over at her. "I know it sounds crazy, but why else would he have come all the way into town the way he did, just to turn around and run home?"

"It doesn't sound crazy." Tessa drove toward town. "It actually makes a lot of sense. I know Harry's saved my hide more than once. Maybe the horse was particularly close to Lisbeth and hoped he could save her. It's a very interesting theory, Cassie. What I'd like to know is why Drake would kill his own sister."

"Or if he did."

"So you're also not convinced he's the one who did it?" Tessa eased off on the gas as she glanced over at her. "The phone just doesn't make sense, right?"

"Yes, exactly." Cassie nodded. "It's odd, isn't it? Why would he kill his sister and then toss his phone right there into the bush?"

"Ollie would probably argue that he just wanted to get rid of it quickly, so he couldn't be tracked." Tessa raised her eyebrows. "But it seems like it was the worst decision he could make if he's a murderer. It makes him look so guilty. He didn't even turn the phone off before he tossed it."

"Maybe the sheer panic was enough to make him not think his choices through." Cassie looked out through the passenger window at the houses they rolled past. "What we need is more information about the whole family. I don't know that much about them. Do you?"

"The Woodcrests?" Tessa smiled and nodded. "Oh, I know quite a bit about them. The Woodcrest boys caused more than their fair share of trouble when I was a cop. Always getting into bad situations, mostly from drinking and hanging around with the wrong crowd. Their mother, Trudy, passed away when they were young. Their father, Stuart, ran the ranch with an iron fist, but it only seemed to make his boys wilder. Both eventually married lovely women and had kids. James had Richard, Lisbeth, and Drake, while Lance had Kim and Jill. But their marriages fell apart, and once the kids were grown, they left Little Leaf Creek behind. Stuart kept running the ranch, and all the grandkids worked there. When he passed away, they were devastated. But when the will was read, things got ugly. He left the ranch to his eldest grandson, Richard, along with Lisbeth and Drake. Their cousins, Kim and Jill, were furious."

"I imagine they would be. I saw the size of that property. It must be worth a fortune."

"It is. The family has a lot of wealth." Tessa continued down the street. "I actually worked a case involving Stuart about twenty years ago. It was huge news back then. Danny, a ranch hand was kidnapped. I wasn't living here at the time, but I was visiting, and they asked me to assist."

"Really? What happened?" Cassie's curiosity piqued.

"Danny was coming back from town late one evening, but the next morning, his truck was found abandoned near the property. The kidnappers thought he was a family member. They demanded a ransom, but Stuart refused to pay. Said it wasn't his responsibility, that he wasn't going to negotiate with criminals."

"That's terrible."

"Danny's family didn't have a penny to their name, so they couldn't do anything. People talked. Some thought Stuart was coldhearted, while others thought he knew something he wasn't saying. Then Danny was returned unharmed. He just packed up and left town not long after. Said he wouldn't work for people who wouldn't help him. His family was so angry with Stuart. Blamed him for Danny leaving town."

"Wow! Were the kidnappers ever caught?" Cassie asked.

"Yes, they were just a couple of drifters who

needed money. It was a case of mistaken identity. They thought Danny was one of Stuart's sons."

"That's crazy." Cassie glanced back over her shoulder and laughed as she dodged a lick from Harry. "You did a good job." She reached over the seat and stroked the top of his head. "If it wasn't for you, they might not have found Lisbeth so quickly."

"Yes, he did good. And we need to get him home, and get you into some clothes." Tessa smiled as she raised one eyebrow. "Before we go to our next stop."

Cassie's cheeks reddened as she realized that she'd spent all this time in her pajamas. She hadn't even considered what she was wearing while she chased down Harry or heard the news about Lisbeth.

"Yes, you're absolutely right. Look at me." Cassie smoothed down her robe. "But what's our next step?"

"Let's ask Mark if he can help us find out more about the family. He always has the inside scoop." Tessa tipped her head toward her phone. "He tried to call me before, so I think he might have already heard what's happened. I think he must have a contact in the Little Leaf Creek Police Department, but he won't tell me who. Go on and call him."

Mark Collingswood was a local lawyer and a good friend of Tessa's. Their friendship had developed into a romantic relationship, even though Tessa would never admit it.

"Sure, I'm sure he can't wait to speak to you." Cassie grinned as she called Mark.

"It's far too early for irritating me, Cassie." Tessa cut a sharp look in her direction.

CHAPTER 5

"Hello? Tessa? Are you okay? I heard what happened, and that Harry was involved?" Mark's voice filled the jeep.

Harry barked a greeting from the back seat.

"We're all okay. Cassie's also here with me." Tessa glanced at her, then continued. "We're hoping to learn more about Lisbeth and her family. Is there anything you can tell us?"

"Not much, really. I probably only know what you would know," Mark said.

"If they had an estate lawyer, that person would likely know a lot about them. Do you have any idea who it is?" Tessa asked.

"Actually, I do. Helen Shipley," Mark said.

"That's great, thank you." Tessa turned onto their street, Little Leaf Way. "Do you know her?"

"Helen? A bit, but we don't run in the same circles. Her offices are in Lockersby. She's been the family's lawyer for years." Mark cleared his throat. "She's had her share of challenges."

"What kind of challenges?" Tessa pulled into her driveway.

"Her husband passed away about fifteen years ago, when her son was just a few years old, and her son caused some trouble a while back. He drove unlicensed and he caused a car crash. He was speeding, and he hit a couple of cyclists. They weren't hurt too badly, but it still turned into a legal and financial nightmare. Helen was left to clean up the mess."

"Okay, thanks, Mark. I'll let you know if I come across anything. And call me if you hear anything important, please?" Tessa ended the call and hopped out of the jeep with Harry, which inspired a series of bleats from the goats who waited just beyond the gate.

"So, what's next?" Cassie asked.

"We need to hurry up and see Helen. If the police talk to her before us, and she has anything to hide, she'll already be well on her way to covering it up."

"Cassie!" Sebastian called out to her from their side of the gate. "I just popped back to get something. Can I get a quick update?"

"Sure." Cassie smiled. "Tessa, I'll be right back."

"I'll get Harry settled and find Helen's address." Tessa rushed inside to fill Harry's bowls with food and water.

Cassie hurried through the gate to her own driveway and pulled Sebastian into a warm hug. "Come with me. I'll tell you everything while I change."

As promised, Cassie filled him in on every detail while she changed into a T-shirt and jeans.

"So, you chased a horse?" Sebastian watched her rush past him to grab her shoes.

"And a dog!"

"And discovered a dead body?"

"Yes, it was pretty eventful and shocking." Cassie's voice softened.

"And I guess now you want to figure out what happened to her." Sebastian opened his arms to her.

"Yes." Cassie nestled into his arms and closed her eyes. For several seconds, she savored his warmth around her, but a not-so-subtle beep of a horn from outside stirred her from his soothing embrace. "I'm sorry. Tessa's waiting. We're going to see what we can find out about the family's legal and financial history."

"You do that, and while I'm out making the deliveries, I'll see what I can find out about the Woodcrests and their ranch. A lot of the big property owners have their own little club. I might be able to find out something that might be helpful." Sebastian walked her out to the front porch, kissed her, then watched as she walked over to the jeep.

Cassie climbed into the jeep and gave Tessa a pointed look. "Was the beeping really necessary?"

"Not really." Tessa flashed her a smile. "But I don't get to use the horn that often. I already have directions set up to go to Helen's office." She started the jeep and backed out of the driveway. "And I managed to get some info from the medical examiner. He's still at the scene, so he couldn't tell me much, but he estimates her time of death was between about five and six this morning, and she was stabbed with a hay hook."

"So, the murder might not have been planned. You would find a hay hook in a barn, right?"

"Right."

"Sebastian's going to ask around about the

Woodcrests, to see if he can find out more about them and their ranch." Cassie pulled out her phone and began her own search as Tessa headed down the highway that led to the much larger town.

As they turned onto the main road in Lockersby, Cassie looked at Tessa. "It looks like the only posts that Lisbeth recently made were related to the horses. Especially the silver one. His name's Phantom. She loved him very much."

"I'm glad he got back home safe." Tessa turned off the main road and into the parking lot of a small office building.

"Me, too. So, what do you expect to find out from Helen?" Cassie asked.

"I'm not sure, exactly. But she probably knows some of the juicy family secrets. Whether she'll share any with us is the question, and whether she'll be honest with us or not, is the bigger question." Tessa parked in front of the building's entrance, then turned the engine off.

"I'm sure she'll want to do whatever she can to help us." Cassie stepped out of the jeep.

Tessa met her on the sidewalk in front of the building. "I wish I were as certain as you are. In case you haven't noticed, I don't exactly trust lawyers."

"Except Mark."

"Except Mark." Tessa pursed her lips. "But he's an exception to the rule. Most in this profession are just out to make as much money as they can, and don't have their clients' best interests in mind."

"I don't know if I share that bias." Cassie kept her voice soft as she followed her to Helen's office door. "They're professionals, and without them, we'd be lost trying to sort through all the complicated laws." She stood behind Tessa as they reached the door.

Tessa tried the knob and it turned. "Showtime." She opened the door and stepped inside to find a man, who looked about thirty, with thick brown hair and a serious expression, at the small desk in the front office. "Excuse me, sir, is Helen in, please?" She walked up to the desk with a wide smile.

"Do you have an appointment?" He peered at her suspiciously.

"No, we don't. But we're hoping to have a few minutes to speak with her, if she can spare it?" Tessa turned on her most charming grin as she read his name tag. "Could you please check with her, Allan?"

Cassie recognized Tessa's expression from the many times she'd charmed Mark into sharing more information than he should have.

"I'll check." Allan smiled. "Can I ask who wants to see her? And why?"

Cassie was shocked at how his demeanor changed so quickly.

"Tessa and Cassie." Tessa gestured from herself to Cassie. "We wanted to talk to her about the Woodcrests."

"You two take a seat. I'll check if she can see you." Allan picked up his phone.

"Thank you so much." Tessa smiled before she dropped down into one of the chairs lining the far wall of the small space.

Cassie joined her while doing her best to hold back a grin. Seeing Tessa in charming mode always surprised and impressed her.

"She has a few minutes to spare." Allan hung up the phone. "You can go ahead in." He pointed down the hall.

Tessa took the lead as they walked in that direction.

CHAPTER 6

On the way down a short hallway, Cassie could smell the scent of fragrant flowers. The closer she came to Helen's office, the thicker the scent became.

When Tessa opened the office door, an entire cloud of the smell drifted outward to greet them both.

Tessa's nose crinkled as she pushed through it and entered the office, then signaled for Cassie to join her. "I'm Tessa, and this is Cassie. Thanks for seeing us, Helen. I know this must be a difficult time for you."

A woman who appeared to be in her late forties looked up at them as she swept her platinum-blonde hair back over the shoulders of her steel-gray business suit. "A shocking time, that's for sure." She scooted her office chair closer to her desk. "I still don't understand what happened, and it sure seems as if the police are dragging their feet to get this situation solved."

"It only just happened. I'm sure they're hard at work trying to get to the truth." Cassie settled in the chair across from her and casually glanced around as she tried to find the source of the scent. "Any information you gave them about the family was probably very helpful."

"Not a word." Helen folded her arms across her chest. "The moment I saw the badge, I let them know they would need a warrant. I'm not someone who will simply turn over the personal details of my clients' lives."

"But it's a murder investigation." Cassie studied her. "I would think you would want to give them all the information they might need to figure out who did this to Lisbeth."

"It's their job to find that information, not my job to provide it." Helen's shoulders slumped. "I know it sounds cold. But if every lawyer gave away personal information to every police officer who asked, we'd never have the trust of our clients again."

"I see." Tessa leaned forward and looked into her eyes. "But Lisbeth was murdered? Whoever did this to her needs to be put behind bars."

"It's tragic, yes. But that doesn't mean they get to see all the records, or get personal information from me." Helen leaned back in her chair. "I'm not being difficult. I'm upholding my duty to my clients."

"Of course. You take your job very seriously." Tessa pulled her chair closer to the desk. "But we're not the police. Can you tell us a little bit about Drake? And Lisbeth? We just want to get to know the family a little better."

"Are you asking me if I think Drake killed his sister?" Helen sat back in her chair and stared across the desk at both of them. "You can just come out and ask, if that's what you want to know."

"Yes, that's what we want to know." Tessa nodded. "I think that's what the whole town wants to know, as well as where Drake might be hiding out."

"The answer's no." Helen drew her lips into a hard straight line as she stared at them both for a long moment before she continued. "I know that may not be what you want to hear, but Drake isn't a murderer. If you had said Richard, I might believe you. He's always in a desperate financial situation. But Lisbeth practically raised Drake. There's no way that he would turn against her. If that's what you think, you're really off the mark."

"Well, what are we supposed to think?" Tessa gazed back at her. "Lisbeth is dead. And Drake's phone was found in the bushes near the barn where she was killed, and now he's nowhere to be found. It sounds like he might be on the run, to me. Was anything out of the ordinary recently? Did Drake turn to you for extra cash?"

"No, nothing. Drake didn't come to me for anything. And if he did, Lisbeth would have had to approve it as well. After what she'd gone through with Richard draining the funds, we recently agreed that nothing would come out of the account without her approval." Helen flinched. "I guess that's going to have to change now."

"How was Richard draining the funds?" Tessa asked.

"He was withdrawing small amounts here and there, and claimed it was for the ranch, which he was technically entitled to, but it turned out he was using it for personal expenses. It all added up. Lisbeth was furious when she found out the extent of it. He couldn't use the funds that way. The money was meant for the three siblings to invest into the property, themselves, or their education." Helen tapped her finger against her desk. "Stuart was very specific about how he wanted his money to be used."

"But he didn't leave everything to Richard, Drake, and Lisbeth, did he?" Cassie pulled a small notebook from her purse where she'd made a few notes already that morning. "He had two other granddaughters, right? Jill and Kim?"

"Yes. He left the ranch to Lisbeth and her brothers, but he did leave some money for Jill and Kim as well." Helen pursed her lips. "The day that will was read was a very difficult one."

"Did he tell you why he didn't leave some of the ranch to his other grandchildren? Did they have some kind of falling out?" Cassie asked.

"Now, you're getting into very personal territory." Helen sighed. "Listen, I can't tell you every detail, but let's just say that Stuart had a favorite grandchild, his granddaughter."

"And that favorite granddaughter wasn't Jill or Kim." Tessa gave a slight nod. "They must have been very angry and hurt."

"They were, although I have to admit I found it surprising they were so upset. They received a large inheritance. So, it wasn't as if they were completely left out. They just didn't get a portion of the ranch. But you know how it is. No one's ever satisfied." Helen sat back in her chair. "I've already said more than I should have, and that's all I'm going to say about it. I'm sorry I can't be of more help."

"Okay, thank you for speaking with us." Tessa stood up.

"I just wish this had never happened." Helen closed her eyes for a moment, then opened them again and gestured to a large candle in a glass jar. "I lit it the moment I heard about Lisbeth's death, and I've been burning it ever since. It's not much, but it's something, right?" She inhaled the flowery scent the candle gave off. "It reminds me of her. No matter where she was, it was like she brought the scent of nature right along with her."

"It's lovely." Cassie met her eyes. "We're going to do what we can to find out what happened to her."

"As will I." Helen turned her attention to the pile of papers on her desk.

Once they were outside the office, Tessa leaned close to Cassie. "I think we should visit Lisbeth's cousins." Tessa quickened her pace as she neared the jeep. "No matter how much money Stuart left them, it's obvious they felt slighted by not getting a share of the ranch. That might be enough motive for one or both of them to murder Lisbeth."

CHAPTER 7

"Let's use a little caution when we speak with Kim and Jill." Cassie surveyed the apartment building that Tessa rolled toward. "It hasn't been long since Lisbeth was killed. They may still be in shock."

"You're right. We do need to consider their grief in all this. But the sooner we speak with them, the better the chance we'll discover something that can help us solve this. The shock of losing a loved one can be overwhelming, but it can also sharpen the mind in some ways. Let's just find out what we can, without making things worse on them. They're in number five, right over there." Tessa stepped out of the jeep and began walking toward the apartment.

Cassie trailed a few steps behind. She tried to

imagine whether a cousin would really be so resentful over an inheritance, that murder would be an option. If Kim and Jill were involved in Lisbeth's death, what did that mean for Drake? Could he really be hurt, or worse? And what about Chase? Where were they?

Tessa knocked on the door. A few seconds later, it swung open.

"Yes? Can I help you?" A woman in her late twenties or early thirties with a short brunette bob and dark brown eyes looked between them.

"I'm Cassie, and this is my friend Tessa. We're so sorry for your loss."

"Oh. It's so awful, isn't it?" She took a step back. "Come in. I'm Jill, and this is my sister, Kim."

Another woman around the same age, maybe a bit younger, waved to them from the couch. As she did, Cassie noticed what looked like a few pieces of hay clinging to the back of the sleeve of her sweater. Her lighter and longer hair stood out against her sister's, but their eyes appeared to be the same shade.

"We've been expecting you." Jill walked farther inside.

"You have?" Cassie stepped into the living room.

"Yes. Helen told us you'd been to see her, and

since we already spoke to the police we figured you'd be here next. What I don't understand is why?" Jill looked straight at Cassie. "Are you here to accuse us of murder, too?"

"What?" Cassie's eyes widened as she shook her head. "No, not at all. We were just hoping you might be able to tell us a little bit more about Lisbeth, and Drake. Maybe you can offer some insight. Tessa's a retired detective, so she might be able to help get to the bottom of this as quickly as possible."

Kim spoke up from the couch. "I don't know how to even process it. I just can't seem to accept it. And the idea that they think Drake might be involved?" She grabbed a tissue from a box on the coffee table and began dabbing at her eyes. "I just can't even imagine that."

"I guess that's why we're really here, to make sense of it all." Tessa watched as Jill began pacing back and forth across the room.

"But that's the thing. It doesn't make any sense. Drake and Lisbeth were never the ones who fought with each other." Kim crossed her arms. "Richard and Lisbeth would butt heads for sure. But not Drake. There's no way he killed her."

"How can you be so sure? Siblings fight

sometimes. Issues come up that you might not expect. Maybe she said something that really upset him?" Cassie suggested.

"She practically raised him. Drake's the baby of the family. Jill and I were toddlers when he was born. But Lisbeth was already eight, and Richard was ten. Lisbeth became like his little mother, especially when their mother already had one foot out the door. Not unlike our own." Kim glanced at her sister. "They weren't exactly the good old days, were they?"

"With Lisbeth, they were." Jill smiled. "She wasn't just nurturing with Drake. She looked out for us, too. Really, she was responsible for most of our good childhood memories."

"Look, the family had ups and downs, just like all families experience." Kim let out a deep breath. "But certainly nothing that would lead to murder."

"So, you really don't believe that Drake would hurt her? Could he have been involved with drugs or something of that nature?" Tessa raised her eyebrows. "People can be unpredictable, if they're suffering from addiction."

"No, nothing like that. We weren't close anymore, but we would have known if he was caught up in something that bad." Jill sighed.

"Listen, I truly believe that you're just here to help get to the bottom of this, but honestly my sister and I need some time to grieve and to accept what's happened. We really can't keep answering the same questions over and over again."

"I understand." Cassie nodded, then glanced over at Tessa. "We'll be on our way."

"But if you need anything at all, please let us know." Tessa handed Jill a card with her number on it.

"Sure, we will." Jill followed them to the door. "Just do me a favor and look for Drake. I know he's not on the run. I just hope he's still alive. Maybe he's been hurt. Maybe he's out there somewhere, overwhelmed by what happened to Lisbeth. Please." She looked into Tessa's eyes. "We don't want to lose him, too."

"We'll update you as soon as we know anything," Tessa said.

"Thank you. And thank you for being so kind. I know there's a murder to solve, but right now all we can think about is our loss and making sure Drake's okay, not how it happened, or who did it." Jill's voice wavered.

"We understand." Cassie held her gaze a moment longer before she continued out the door.

"They were so upset. It's terrible." She hopped into the jeep.

"It is. But over the years, I've learned that sometimes people use grief as a way to hide their guilt."

Stunned by those words, Cassie started to argue the point, but her cell phone began ringing before she could. She didn't recognize the number at first and hesitated to answer. Suddenly she recalled jotting the number down in her notebook.

"I think it's Richard. Maybe he's found Drake." She answered the call. "Richard?"

"It's Drake," Richard mumbled into the phone. "He's not on the run. He's been kidnapped!"

CHAPTER 8

"What?" Cassie narrowed her eyes as Richard's words echoed in her ears. "What do you mean Drake's been kidnapped? How do you know?"

"I just found a ransom note." Richard's voice trembled. "It says that if I don't get the money they want, they're going to kill Drake, too."

"Did you tell the police?" Cassie's heart pounded as Tessa glanced over at her with wide, curious eyes. "If you received a ransom note, you need to tell them immediately."

"No. I can't. The note says absolutely no police. If I tell them, the kidnapper's going to kill Drake right away. Please, I need you and Tessa to help. I know you both often help solve the crimes around here. I'm at home. Can you come here and help me get Drake back, please. I've already lost Lisbeth. I can't let anything happen to Drake."

"Okay, Richard, we're on our way." Cassie's heart raced. "We'll be there soon. Just stay right where you are. Don't do anything, and don't speak to anyone, okay?"

"Okay, but I'm going to hang up in case the kidnapper tries to call. Get here fast. I have no idea what to do." Richard ended the call.

"Did I hear that right?" Tessa stepped on the gas. "Did he say Drake's been kidnapped and he received a ransom note?"

"Yes, and it says absolutely no police can be involved."

"Tell Ollie." Tessa swung around a corner and stepped on the gas again, headed straight for the ranch.

"I know we have to tell him." Cassie cradled her phone in her hands. "But do you think it will put Drake at risk?"

"Ollie knows what he's doing. He can be very discreet about the whole situation. Just text him about what we know so far."

"Okay." Cassie typed out a quick text emphasizing the need to keep things quiet. "I trust

Ollie, of course. I just worry he has to follow protocol. If Drake was abducted, what are the chances they'll get him back safely?"

"I'm not sure he was abducted." Tessa turned onto the long dirt driveway. Police cars still surrounded the barn which remained cordoned off with bright yellow police tape. "I think it's odd that Richard would call us first instead of asking any of the officers here for help."

"Yes, I guess it is odd. But the note did say not to involve the police. And he just mentioned that he knows we investigate things, and maybe he thinks you can help because you're an ex-cop." Cassie tried to slow down her racing heart. "It makes sense that Drake was taken, since his phone was tossed into the bushes, and his truck is still here."

"It does." Tessa peered through the windshield at Richard who paced back and forth across the long front porch that stretched the length of his house. "But why the delay in the ransom note?"

"No idea, but maybe it'll give us some clues."

"This would be the second abduction the Woodcrests have been involved in, that I know of, at least."

"Quite a coincidence." Cassie climbed out of the jeep and headed straight for the porch.

"Thanks for coming." Richard rushed toward them as they approached. "I didn't know what else to do. I thought you could help, Tessa, given your experience. The ransom note said not to contact the police."

"I understand that it said that." Tessa looked into his eyes. "But you have to know that the best thing to do is to let the police investigate this. They have all the resources that will be needed to figure out who has Drake and where they have him."

"No. No, please!" Richard pleaded. "Listen to me, I can't lose another sibling today. Do you hear me? I can't. I just can't."

"Okay, okay. Just relax." Cassie patted the air. "Why don't you start by showing us the note, and telling us where you found it?"

Richard glanced toward the barn where a couple of officers still milled about while the crime scene investigation team gathered evidence.

"Come with me, around the back." Richard led them along a walkway that wound around the side of the house to a hedged garden. He stopped beside a bench near a large maple tree and pointed to a note pinned to it. "It's there. I sit here every day. I needed to try and clear my head with everything going on, and sitting here helps me with that. When I came here, I found it."

"It's a risky place to leave a note. They must have presumed you would definitely come out here, and they're familiar with your daily habits." Tessa turned slowly to take in the isolated spot in the garden.

"This is the area where we would always play as kids. We loved coming out here." Richard stared at the note. "It says that if I don't produce four hundred thousand dollars, they're going to kill Drake, like they killed Lisbeth." He groaned as he squeezed his eyes shut. "I don't have that kind of money. What am I going to do? I'll have to find it somehow, but it takes time to sell things. And the money isn't just sitting in our trust account. It's not like I can just snap my fingers and make it happen."

"Let's slow down for a moment." Tessa's even tone drew his attention. "I know you're worried, but being worried isn't what's going to bring Drake home. We need to consider all aspects of this with as clear a mind as possible. Is there anything about the writing on the note that seems familiar to you? It was handwritten. Do you recognize the writing? The phrasing?"

"What? Why would I?" Richard glared at Tessa.

"Do you really believe that whoever did this is someone we know?"

"Yes, yes, I do." Tessa studied the note. "I think it's someone who knows all of you quite well. They knew enough to put the note in a place that you would go to seek comfort. They knew enough to find Lisbeth in the barn early this morning. Whoever did this is very likely close to the family." She shifted her gaze back to Richard. "That's why you need to clear your mind and think. You may very well hold the key to who's responsible."

"I can't," Richard groaned and covered his face. "I can't even think straight."

"Try to breathe. A few nice, slow breaths." Oliver's voice caused Richard to drop his hands instantly and take a large step back.

"What's he doing here?" Richard's eyes widened at the sight of Oliver a few feet away from him. "Did you tell him?"

"We did." Tessa held up her hands. "But don't worry, Oliver's a professional. He knows how to keep things under wraps and not let the kidnapper know that he's involved. And he made sure not to tell any of the other officers, just in case there are any leaks. Trust me, Richard, with his help we're going to get to the truth much faster. We need to figure out who did this. We need to get Drake to safety as soon as possible."

"I can tell you who it was." Richard's voice raised. "It's that criminal she hired to help take care of the horses. I told her that it was a ridiculous idea to hire someone with a record, but she insisted that he deserved a second chance." His anger faded as tears filled his eyes. "She was always like that, so good to people. Too good for this world." He sniffled. "I can't believe this is how he repaid her. And he has Drake!" His hands balled into fists. "I'll never let him get away with this."

"Wait. Are you talking about Chase? The ranch hand?" Oliver narrowed his eyes. "I still haven't been able to locate him to question him."

"I bet you haven't. Because he's holed up somewhere with my brother." Richard turned and glared at the note. "He wants money. That's why he did this."

"Richard!" a voice bellowed from the front of the house. It came again, growing closer, as the person rounded the house to reach the garden.

"That's him." Richard scowled. "Chase! What have you done?"

A young man with a thick, muscular build, and an ample helping of wavy blond hair that nearly reached his shoulders, stepped around the side of the house and strode straight toward them. "Richard, what's going on? Where's Lisbeth?"

"Chase?" Oliver shifted into his path before he could reach Richard. "I've been calling and texting you all morning."

"You have? I don't answer numbers I don't recognize and I didn't notice the texts." Chase looked Oliver over. His plain clothes disguised his profession, but the badge on his belt caught Chase's attention. "What's happened?"

"As if you don't know." Richard raised his voice as he took a step toward Chase.

"Just relax." Tessa stepped in front of him.

"Richard, this is only going to make things worse." Cassie softened her tone. "Let him tell us what he knows. We have to find Drake!"

CHAPTER 9

"*D*rake?" A bewildered expression crossed Chase's face. "Where's Lisbeth? Is she okay? I was at my girlfriend's place, I didn't know about any of this."

"No." Richard looked into his eyes. "She's dead. But you know that, because you killed her. Where's my brother, Chase?"

"What are you saying?" Chase snapped.

"Calm down, both of you." Oliver kept his tone soft but authoritative. "This isn't going to help the investigation or get Drake back."

"I don't understand. Where's Drake? What happened to Lisbeth?" Chase's eyes darted from person to person.

"We were hoping you might be able to give us

some insight into that." Oliver pointed at the note on the tree. "Do you know anything about this?"

"Is that a ransom note?" Chase's eyes widened, then brimmed with tears. "Are you saying this is real? Lisbeth is really dead?"

"Yes, she's dead." Richard's voice faltered.

Cassie wanted to offer Chase comfort, but a million questions ran through her mind.

"Don't you normally work with Lisbeth? Why weren't you at the barn with her this morning?" Cassie blurted out.

"Lisbeth gave me the morning off." Chase swallowed hard. "It was my girlfriend's birthday, yesterday, so Lisbeth said I can start later." He looked over his shoulder in the direction of the barn. "It happened in the barn? I don't understand. Who would want to kill Lisbeth?"

"We were hoping you might be able to give us some ideas." Tessa took a step toward him. "You must know quite a bit about her. You two worked closely together. Had she been upset with anyone recently?"

"No, no one." Chase narrowed his eyes. "Lisbeth was kind to everyone."

"That's all we keep hearing." Oliver settled his hand on his belt. "But someone disliked her enough to murder her, and it looks like they've abducted her brother as well. I don't think this is just about money. I believe it was personal. So, who has she spent time with lately?"

"No one." Chase shoved his hands into his jeans' pockets, then abruptly looked up at Oliver. "Well, there's Gordon. He owns the property next door. I know she'd met with him a few times lately."

"Met with him about what?" Oliver asked.

"I'm not sure. At first, I thought maybe something romantic was going on, even though he's much older than her, but the way she spoke about him made me think it was more about business." Chase tilted his head slightly. "I didn't question her. I was just glad she took a chance on me and hired me."

"If I find out you did anything to hurt her, Chase, I swear there will be consequences." Richard took a step toward him and pointed a finger in his face.

"That's enough." Oliver's stern tone caused Richard to freeze where he stood and lower his hand. "Chase, I think it would be best if you come down to the station with me to discuss this."

"Sure, whatever you need." Chase ruffled his hand through his hair. "I just can't believe this. Why

Lisbeth? She never did anything to anyone." He followed Oliver toward the car.

Cassie watched as Oliver put Chase in the back seat, then she turned to face Tessa and Richard.

"I told Lisbeth not to hire him after the trouble we had with Brody, but she just saw the best in everyone." Richard sighed.

"Who's Brody?" Tessa asked.

"Brody Foster. An old school friend of Drake's. He lived with us for a while about a year back when he needed a place to stay, but he's bad news, always has been. Once a criminal, always a criminal, if you ask me. Drake eventually stopped spending time with him and ended up banning him from the property," Richard said.

"Do you think he could have had something to do with this?" Tessa searched her memory for someone named Brody, but no one came to mind.

"I don't know." Richard's shoulders slumped. "I don't know what he's been up to lately, but I wouldn't be surprised if he got involved in something shady."

"What did he do to get banned?" Tessa took a step closer to him.

"He had a record, some charges for theft." Richard clenched his hands into fists. "But the real issue was that things kept disappearing when he was around, tools, money, even some of Grandad's old valuables from the house. We could never prove anything, but we were sure he was behind it."

"Did he threaten Drake when he told him to stay away?" Cassie pressed.

"Not in so many words. But he wasn't happy," Richard said.

Tessa and Cassie exchanged a quick glance.

"When was the last time you saw him?" Cassie pulled out her notebook.

"A couple of months ago, maybe longer. He tried to stop by a few times, but Lisbeth and Drake turned him away." Richard paused, then gave his head a quick shake as if to clear his thoughts. "My mind is so fuzzy with all of this. I forgot that a few days ago, Drake said he thought he saw him hanging around on the property near the barn."

"Did he report it?" Tessa asked.

"No. By the time Drake got to the barn he'd disappeared. He wasn't sure it was him." Richard glanced in the direction of the barn.

"Do you think he's capable of murder?" Cassie met his gaze.

"Maybe. I wouldn't put it past him." Richard shrugged.

"Where would we find him now?" Tessa studied him as she wondered if he was just trying to divert suspicion.

"Last I heard, he was staying at an apartment in Lockersby but I have no idea if he's still there. I don't know the address."

"We'll see if we can find him. You should get some rest." Tessa gestured to the house.

"Okay." Richard started toward the porch, then glanced over his shoulder. "You'll let me know if you find out anything."

"Yes, of course." Tessa turned toward Cassie. "We need to be open to all possibilities, but I think we can assume that the person or people who killed Lisbeth, kidnapped Drake as well."

"That's what I was thinking."

"I know Chase is being questioned at the moment, but we can't rely on the fact that he did this." Tessa walked back over to the jeep. "And now we have some other avenues to investigate."

"Where do you want to start?" Cassie asked.

"I think we'll go over and talk to Gordon. He's just next door. Chase claims Lisbeth had been seeing him more often lately. Maybe he knows something. Let's see what he has to say."

"You're right. We have to find the people who

were closest to Lisbeth, and people who might have seen her recently." Cassie opened the passenger side door. "Something still feels off to me about finding the note that way." She climbed in. "But it's going to take some time for me to sort all of that out."

"What surprises me the most is that either the note was overlooked by the police on the first search of the property, which is possible but seems unlikely, or the kidnapper was bold enough to enter the property after the murder and abduction had already taken place, and put the note on that tree." Tessa navigated down the driveway and turned down the road toward the next property.

"And why kill her, then? Why kill her in the barn when she was tending to the horses? Why not before or after? And how did they know Drake would be there, too?"

"Exactly." Tessa turned down the next long driveway, this one leading to a much more manicured property, less ranch and more mansion. "Which once again indicates to me that someone familiar with the ranch and Lisbeth's schedule probably committed these crimes. This wasn't just a stranger who wandered onto the property. And now, with the ransom note, it's clear that whoever's behind this, whether one person or more, intended to get money out of the situation."

"But if all they wanted was money, why didn't they just take Lisbeth? Why did they kill her?"

"I guess it's possible that the killer targeted Lisbeth to abduct her, but Drake interrupted and she ended up dead." Tessa stepped out of the jeep and met Cassie around the front. "But, I don't know. Maybe it wasn't just about the money."

"Hopefully, Gordon can clarify a few things for us." Cassie followed Tessa toward the expansive house.

CHAPTER 10

Tessa reached Gordon's front door and rang the doorbell.

A few minutes slipped by, and Cassie looked up at a camera that pointed at the area just outside the door. "Maybe he isn't home."

Tessa reached for the button again, but the door swung open before she pressed it.

"Yes?" The slender man in the doorway stared out at them. His long, dark hair hung forward in his face, disguising most of it from view.

"Gordon?" Cassie peered at him. "I'm Cassie and this is Tessa. We're just here to ask you a few questions about your neighbor Lisbeth."

"Are you the police?" Gordon focused on Tessa. "I thought you were retired."

"No, we're not the police. I retired a long time ago." Tessa had seen him around town over the years but had never formally met him. "But we're trying to help figure out what happened at the ranch."

"I see. Sure, you can ask me whatever you want, but I don't think I can be much help. The police just left here. They told me Lisbeth was murdered. I can't believe it." Gordon frowned.

"Did you notice anything unusual this morning? Did you hear anything? Maybe see a horse running past your place?" Cassie asked.

"No, nothing like that." Gordon shook his head. "I had a very early shoot this morning, so I was out before five."

"A shoot?" Cassie studied him. He appeared to be in his fifties, but he had a very lean and youthful appearance. "Are you some kind of model?"

"A model?" Gordon laughed, a spark lit up his eyes. "Not at all. It was a commercial for my company. They wanted the CEO to be part of the advertisement. I protested, but you know how it is when the younger generation runs the show. They get what they want?"

"Oh, what's your company?" Cassie glanced around the well-decorated entryway.

"I run an investment firm that works with people from all walks of life." Gordon pulled a business card from his pocket and offered it to Cassie. "You should get in touch. A lot of people think that investments are out of their reach, but it's a lot simpler than you may think."

"Thanks." Cassie took the card from him and slipped it into her pocket. She tried not to be offended, as he'd just assumed she had no idea about investing. "So, then you don't know about anything that happened at your neighbor's place this morning?"

"No, no idea. When I drove past and I saw the police lights at the house, I just presumed Richard had gotten Lisbeth into trouble again." Gordon's eyes darkened.

"Why would you think that Richard would get her into trouble?" Tessa asked.

"Oh, he was always causing her problems. He might be the oldest sibling, but he's the most irresponsible. He's got a business degree, but he can't keep a job for more than a week. Every time Lisbeth turned around he'd sold another heirloom." Gordon looked between them. "I think she wanted something positive to focus on. That's why she was opening a horse-riding school. They board horses and own a few, and she really wanted to expand and start the school. I wouldn't normally invest in a start-up like that, but she needed a little capital for it, so I offered to help her out. I made a small investment."

"Can you tell us more about it?" Cassie asked.

"Sure, I can tell you some. But to be honest, she didn't give me very many details. That was my mistake. I assumed that she was a businesswoman, but I came to think that she may have been guessing at how to start the business." Gordon leaned against the doorway. "She had such a wonderful idea. She wanted it to be accessible to people of all incomes, all abilities. She'd been working with the horses and training them for some time. She claimed to already have several students lined up, but she needed money for more stables, new equipment, and to get all the stables and rings up to par with government regulations." He looked up at both of them. "She was so passionate about this idea, I guess I was just swept up in it." He glanced over his shoulder, into the house. "I'm sorry, I wish I could help you more, but I have a business call scheduled. And I still need to process this terrible news."

"You left early this morning?" Tessa looked straight into his eyes.

"Yes, well before sunrise, at about four thirty." Gordon took a step inside and closed the door.

Tessa led the way back to the jeep. "I'd hoped he'd have a little more to tell us."

"Me, too." Cassie glanced back over her shoulder at the house. "He didn't seem very upset that she was dead, did he?"

"No, not very. But people react differently. It might not have sunk in yet." Tessa slid into the driver's seat. "I'm going to text Ollie to see if he checked Gordon's alibi."

"Do you really think he could be involved?" Cassie buckled into the seat beside her.

"He did loan her money. I get the feeling he's not being completely honest about their relationship, either. Why would he take a chance on her when he said himself that's not something he would normally do?"

"I'm not sure, but if there's something to find out, we're not going to find it out now. He was eager to get us out of here."

"He was." Tessa held up her phone with a text on display. "Mark managed to track down Brody's apartment in Lockersby for us."

"Should we go and have a conversation with him?"

"Absolutely." Tessa hopped into the jeep.

CHAPTER 11

*T*essa pulled into a parking spot outside the apartment complex and turned off the engine. She hopped out and led the way to apartment 10.

"This is it." Tessa knocked firmly. When there was no response, she knocked again, louder this time. "Brody, we just want to talk."

An older man from a neighboring apartment leaned over the balcony railing and called down to them. "You're looking for Brody?"

Tessa looked up at him. "Yes. Do you know if he's home?"

The man shook his head. "Hasn't been here all day. He does long hours at the new nursery in town."

"Thanks." Tessa exchanged a glance with Cassie before heading back to the jeep.

A short drive later, Tessa pulled into a parking spot outside the small plant nursery. "Let's hope this is the right place and Brody's here." She turned off the engine and climbed out.

Cassie followed her toward the front counter.

Tessa smiled at the young woman behind it. "We're looking for Brody."

"In the greenhouse." She pointed in the direction as she snapped her gum.

Tessa led the way to the large glass structure, its panes slightly fogged from the warmth and humidity inside. Rows of potted plants lined the interior. A man in a staff uniform was hunched over a workbench as he sorted through a tray of seedlings. A sign on the door read Staff Only.

Tessa tried the door but it was locked. She rapped on the glass. The man stiffened, but he didn't turn toward them, and continued working.

Cassie crossed her arms. "He's definitely avoiding us."

Tessa knocked again, harder this time. The man let out a visible sigh before straightening. He hesitated, then finally made his way to the door. Instead of unlocking it right away, he just stood there, as if debating whether to send them away.

After a long pause, he finally slid the lock and cracked the door open a bit. His expression was wary. "What?"

"Brody." Tessa confirmed it was him from his name tag. "We just need a moment of your time, please. We just have a couple of questions for you."

"About what?" Brody continued to look through the narrow opening.

"About Lisbeth." Tessa watched his reaction.

"About her murder? I just heard about it. I knew someone would be after me because of it." Brody scowled. "I don't know anything. And I don't talk to the police."

"We aren't the police. If you had nothing to do with this, we can help clear your name." Tessa softened her tone. "If we found out about your history with the family, the police will, too."

"Look, I didn't kill Lisbeth, but I knew this would come back on me. She never liked me. She thought I was a thief." Brody ran a hand through his hair.

"Were you?" Tessa crossed her arms.

"Maybe I took a couple of things, but it was because I helped out around the ranch and they never paid me. They had so much." Brody shrugged. "They could never need it all, and I could barely rub two pennies together. But, no matter what I did, I had nothing to do with any of this. I swear, I wasn't anywhere near Little Leaf Creek this morning. I heard that's when she was killed."

"If it wasn't you, do you have any idea who it could have been?" Tessa asked.

"Maybe Kim and Jill. Their cousins. They were so angry that they didn't get some of the ranch." Brody looked between them. "But I really can't believe they killed her."

"Anyone else?" Tessa asked.

Brody shifted from foot to foot, then glanced around before lowering his voice. "I shouldn't even be talking to you here. I just got this job. Things are starting to look up for me, and the last thing I need is people thinking I'm involved in something like this."

"Who is it?" Tessa tried to meet his eyes. "I can tell there's someone."

"Norman." Brody sighed.

"Norman?" Tessa searched her memory for who he might be talking about. As she placed the name, he spoke up.

"Danny's dad. That guy who was kidnapped

from the ranch years ago. Do you know about that?" Brody brushed the dirt from his jeans.

"Yes. What about it?" Tessa was eager to find out what he had to say.

"Well, Norman's always held a grudge against the family because Stuart never paid the ransom to have Danny released. But Norman's kept pretty quiet about it lately. That is, until the other night." Brody nodded. "I saw him at the bar. He'd been drinking too much, and since he knew I had a bad history with the family, he started ranting. He was shouting about how he was going to get back at them for driving his son away. He was furious."

"Are you sure?" Tessa's mind raced. "After all this time?"

"Absolutely! I don't know why, but something brought it all to the surface again. To be honest, though, he's a frail old man. I couldn't imagine him doing this himself. He doesn't have any family in the area anymore." Brody took a step back farther inside. "I had nothing to do with this, and I don't want to point any fingers, but if you kill someone, you need to do your time. I'm not saying he did it, but I would definitely look into him." He closed the door.

Cassie followed Tessa out of the nursery and

toward the jeep, as they tried to process the information.

"Do you believe him?" Cassie turned toward her.

"I don't know. He seemed all too willing to throw someone else under the bus. I'm going to see if Mark can look into it for me." Tessa hopped into the driver's seat and typed out a text to Mark.

Cassie glanced at her phone, then gasped. "Oh, wow, I didn't realize what time it was, or even what day it is." She blinked a few times, then wiped her hand across her forehead. "I feel like it's been a week, when it's only been a few hours. I have a shift at the diner. Why don't you come with me? You can get something to eat, and we can see if we can overhear any interesting info. It will probably be busy with everyone wanting to discuss what happened."

Cassie fired off a quick text to Mirabel assuring her that she would be arriving soon.

"Good idea. I am hungry." Tessa turned onto the highway in the direction of Little Leaf Creek. "You know, I've been thinking about what Gordon said. I wonder if the riding school might have something to do with what happened this morning. Richard's in debt. What if he argued with his sister, knowing that she'd received money for the school. Maybe he wanted that for himself."

"Yes, and she probably resisted." Cassie imagined the argument unfolding between the siblings. "He would have known she would be in the barn at that time. Maybe he thought it would be the perfect time to confront her because she would be alone. So, he demanded the money, and when she refused, he might have lost it and killed her." She worried her bottom lip. "But how does Drake fit into all of that? Why would Richard abduct his own brother?"

"Maybe he didn't." Tessa stepped on the gas as she continued down the road. "Think about it, Cassie. Richard's in some serious debt, and Lisbeth isn't helping. He's the oldest sibling and probably thinks that he should be in charge of everything. Lisbeth not letting him have access to the trust money might have made him very angry. Maybe that's when he decided to make a plan."

"Okay, I can see him planning to get rid of Lisbeth. But that still doesn't explain what happened to Drake."

"It does if you realize that Lisbeth's death wouldn't automatically give him access to the money. There's two possibilities. Either one, he took

Drake so he could get the ransom money. Or two, Drake was in on the whole thing, and they staged the abduction to get the funds out of their trust account. Maybe they figured that was the only way they could access it." Tessa headed through the center of town toward the diner. "If you ask me, the second option makes more sense than the first."

"Oh, wow." Cassie found it hard to believe. "So, they worked together and killed their sister, so they could get access to the money? Even after everything she did for them?"

"Just because someone seems to be well-liked by everyone around them, that doesn't mean it's true. Often being in the orbit of a very good person leaves you feeling jealous or resentful of the way people applaud them. Especially with Richard's financial struggles, I'd guess that he had quite a bit of jealousy and resentment toward his sister. And he was desperate." Tessa turned into the parking lot of the diner. "I think it's something we should definitely consider. It would explain how the kidnapper knew Lisbeth would be in the barn. The placement of the note. Richard's alibi is being asleep, and Drake's is being kidnapped. See how it all adds up?" She parked.

"Yes, I can see that." Cassie glanced over at her.

"I wish it wasn't a possibility. I hate to think they could do that to her."

"Me, too, but that doesn't mean it isn't true." Tessa stepped out of the jeep.

"Of course, we can't completely discount Jill and Kim, either. They have plenty of reasons to be jealous and resentful of Lisbeth." Cassie led the way toward the diner door.

"You're right. The only difference there is access. But they grew up on the ranch as well, so they're probably just as familiar with it, and Lisbeth's routine. I suppose they could have taken Drake for the same reason, to get Helen to give them money from the trust fund."

CHAPTER 12

When Cassie and Tessa stepped up to the diner door, Cassie reached for the handle, just as the door swung open.

"Oops, sorry." Dr. Jacobs, the local vet, stepped out. Despite being well into his seventies and wearing a cast on his arm, the tall man with broad shoulders had an intimidating presence. "Tessa, Cassie." He looked between them.

"How's your arm coming along?" Tessa pointed at the cast.

"A couple more weeks, and I can finally get this off." Dr. Jacobs flexed the fingers of his broken arm. "I still can't believe I tripped over a bucket. Guess that's what I get for not paying attention." He chuckled. "I was distracted after hearing about that new vet practice opening in Rombsby. Didn't expect competition so close."

"Yes, I was also surprised when I heard about it," Tessa said.

Dr. Jacobs gave a quick shake of his head, dismissing the thought. "Anyway. That's really not important now, is it? Given what's happened." His expression turned more serious. "I heard you were out at the Woodcrest ranch this morning. Are you both okay?"

"We are. Thank you," Tessa said.

Cassie hesitated. She knew she should hurry inside, but curiosity rooted her to the spot. She wanted to know what he had to say.

"How are you?" Tessa asked. "I imagine you knew Lisbeth well?"

"Yes. Very well. I knew her from the day she was born. I've been working on that ranch for years, ever since I opened my practice." Dr. Jacobs' voice cracked as he continued. "I was very good friends with her grandfather, Stuart. We shared a love for horses. I just can't believe this happened. Poor Lisbeth. She was so caring. When I called to check on Richard, he mentioned that you were trying to help."

"We are." Tessa glanced at Cassie. "Do you have any idea who would want to do this to them?"

"No, no idea." Dr. Jacobs shook his head. "I've been at the ranch so many times over the years. Sure, there were issues here and there, as there are with all families and businesses, but nothing like this."

"I'm so sorry." Tessa's gentle tone matched his. "This is just terrible."

"It is." Dr. Jacobs nodded. "And at the worst time, too. Just when she was about to set up the riding school."

"We just heard about it," Tessa said.

"She was so excited. She couldn't stop talking about it." Dr. Jacobs gave a small smile. "She wanted everything to be perfect."

"Were you involved in that at all?" Cassie asked.

"Yes, my practice was going to provide veterinary care for the school." Dr. Jacobs' expression softened. "It was something she and I had talked about for a while, and she was really eager to make it work. My granddaughter, Lynn, was looking forward to being involved, too. She hasn't been here long, but she was excited about the opportunities the school would bring."

"It does sound like it was a great idea." Tessa smiled.

"It was." Dr. Jacobs' phone rang and he slid it out of his pocket. "Sorry, I have to take this. It's the clinic." He glanced at the phone. "Lynn's out at a farm, and I have to get back to work. It was good to see you both." He turned away from them and started down the street toward the veterinary office with his phone to his ear.

"I also better get to work." Cassie opened the diner door and held it for Tessa.

"Thank you." Tessa led the way inside.

Cassie smiled at Mirabel and Stephanie, who stood behind the front counter. "I made it!" She rushed over and grabbed her apron. "Sorry I'm a bit late."

"No problem." Mirabel gave her a quick hug. "I can't believe what happened. Ollie filled me in on all the details he could. And from what I've heard here, it seems like everyone already knows about the kidnapping as well. I think Richard told some people about it, in the quest to get the ransom money, and the news has spread."

"Well, if that's the case, there's no way the kidnapper is going to believe the police aren't involved now," Cassie said.

"Tessa, come sit!" Sebastian waved from a table. "I knew Cassie would come here for her shift. She ran out of the house without breakfast, and I figured you did, too, and I doubt you've had anything to eat. So, I thought I'd meet you here for an update and I can get us some lunch platters."

"That's a great idea." Tessa sat down beside him. "Thank you."

"I have to head out. I have drama class." Stephanie was an aspiring actress. She pulled off her apron and grabbed her purse. "I'll catch up with you later." She headed for the door.

Cassie blew Sebastian a kiss as she finished clocking in, then began tending to the coffeepots behind the counter. "Mirabel, go sit. Take a break. I'll get everyone some coffee and check in on the tables."

"Okay. Thank you. I won't turn down putting my feet up for a couple of minutes, and I'm eager to find out what you and Tessa have found out." Mirabel grinned as she headed over to the table.

After Cassie made sure all the diners had what they needed, she filled up Tessa's and Mirabel's coffee cups as Tessa finished explaining what they'd discovered.

"So, it looks like it wasn't a stranger who killed

her, because of where and when it happened." Sebastian leaned forward. "The way she was killed makes it seem like it wasn't exactly planned. She was stabbed with a hay hook which would have already been in the barn."

"Okay." Mirabel narrowed her eyes. "But how would that lead to Drake being kidnapped? I mean, that must have been planned, right? Maybe the kidnapper went to the barn to kidnap Drake and Lisbeth got in the way?"

"That's if the brothers didn't stage the whole thing," Tessa spoke up.

"That's a definite possibility." Sebastian had a sip of coffee. "Richard called Cassie instead of the police. I know he said that was because he was warned not to call the police and wanted you two to help. But I still find it odd."

"I don't know. Lisbeth seemed to be the only decent person in that family." Mirabel added more sugar to her coffee. "Maybe the brothers are trying to stick together to cover up the murder."

"Exactly." Cassie filled up Sebastian's cup. "That would make sense. The problem is, we have no way to speak to Drake. Maybe if we talk to his cousins again, we can get a few more details about him."

"Yes, that's a good idea, but in the meantime we

have to assume that this was a kidnapping." Tessa tapped her fingertip against the table. "We know that Lisbeth's been killed, and if Drake is in the killer's grasp, we need to get him released as quickly as possible."

CHAPTER 13

Soon after Sebastian and Tessa had left, the diner became hectic, and Cassie and Mirabel barely had a moment to catch their breath.

As the lunch rush started to slow, Mirabel went to pick up Maisy from school and spend time with her before returning for the dinner shift, and Cassie noticed a few people gathered at a booth in the back. They'd been nursing their drinks and getting refills for over an hour. She recognized a few of them, and one in particular stood out.

"Chase?" Cassie walked over to the table, which Mirabel had been serving before she left. "I didn't see you there."

"Cassie." Chase nodded at her, then gestured to

the young woman beside him. "This is my girlfriend, Mallory, and a few of our other friends."

"Nice to meet you, properly." Cassie smiled at Mallory, who came into the diner at least once a week.

"I wish I could say the same about you." Mallory glared at Cassie. "The way I hear it, you think my Chase is a suspect. He even got hauled off to the police station."

"Just for questioning." Cassie looked from her to Chase. "Right, Chase?"

"Right." Chase grabbed Mallory's hand. "Relax, babe, everything's fine. The detective let me go, because he knew he had nothing to hold me on. I have an alibi. I was with you all morning, so I couldn't have done it."

"Anyway, I have no say in who the police take into the station." Cassie noticed a large scratch on Chase's hand as he held Mallory's. "Wow, what happened there?" She pointed at it.

"You know, horses." Chase leaned back against the seat. "It happens sometimes."

"Oh, okay, of course. I'll get you a refill." Cassie picked up his empty glass and walked toward the counter. Her mind churned as she wondered if Richard was right and Chase had killed Lisbeth.

But what motive would he have? He was dependent on her for a job. She'd given him a second chance when others might not have. Why would he kill her?

A few minutes later, Cassie returned the glass filled with soda, just in time to overhear Chase's statement.

"I know exactly who did it." Chase sat back in his chair and looked up into Cassie's eyes as she reached the table. "You can tell your friend, the detective, my friends and I have figured out who did this to Lisbeth, and Drake."

"Oh?" Cassie's eyes widened as she gazed back at him. "Who?"

"That lawyer lady, Helen." Chase gave a firm nod.

"Helen?" Cassie repeated. "Why would she do anything to hurt Lisbeth?"

"I don't know the why exactly, but I do know that Lisbeth didn't trust her, and yesterday evening, before I left work, the last time I saw Lisbeth, she was arguing on the phone with her. Lisbeth said something about the truth coming out. Whatever she was going to spill, Helen decided that it was more important to keep it secret than Lisbeth's life."

"How come you didn't mention this when you

found out Lisbeth was dead? Is that all you know about it? Did Lisbeth tell you what she suspected her of doing?" Cassie raised her eyebrows.

"I was so shocked when I heard about Lisbeth and Drake, I didn't think about it right away. That's all I know about it. That, and my instincts are always right." Chase stood up. "Maybe now the police can leave me alone." He tossed some money down on the table, then he and his friends headed for the door.

Cassie's mind spun as she worked the rest of her shift, wandering between the idea of Helen being involved and Chase trying to deflect guilt. By the time she arrived at Tessa's, she had more questions than answers.

Cassie tossed some carrot pieces to the goats and treats to Harry as she walked through Tessa's yard. She knew that she could never go to Tessa's unprepared, if she expected to get past her pets.

"Tessa." Cassie knocked lightly on the front door, then continued into the house.

"In the kitchen," Tessa called out.

"Do you want to go and see Kim and Jill again?" Cassie walked into the kitchen.

"Yes, but in the morning. It's already late. We're

not going to get anywhere with this tonight. We'll go first thing. I spoke to Ollie, the kidnapper sent a video to Richard to show they have Drake and he looks fine. And he said they're still trying to get the funds together, but the ransom drop is set for late morning tomorrow, so we have time to do some investigating early, unless, of course, this all gets solved overnight. If only he had the manpower to keep an eye on every suspect, but that's not possible. They have to pick their battles. And there are no cameras at the ranch."

Cassie was shocked that it appeared as if Drake really had been kidnapped, but relieved he was apparently okay.

"What are you baking?" Cassie looked over the bowls and ingredients on the kitchen counter.

Tessa loved baking. It helped her sort out her thoughts.

"A cherry pie. In fact, I'm making a few, so we can give them to whoever we need to speak to about all of this. That way we don't have to go over empty-handed." Tessa grabbed the rolling pin from the kitchen drawer. "I still have frozen cherries left from last season, so I might as well put them to good use." She rolled out a sheet of parchment paper. "Oh, and

I think I'll make one for Dr. Jacobs, too. Between falling and breaking his arm and now all this, I think he's really shaken up."

"That's very kind of you, but it seems like a lot of work."

"It is. That's why it's a good thing you're here." Tessa grinned as she held out an apron to her.

"Oh, really?" Cassie laughed. "You've seen and tasted my cooking. This is pretty risky." She slipped the apron around her waist and tied it behind her back.

"You're getting better every day." Tessa winked at her. "And this is a good staple to know. Fruit pies are fairly easy to make. The key is in the crust and the right temperature for baking."

"Okay, I'll do my best." Cassie went over to the sink and washed her hands.

"We'll have to make them in batches, because they won't all fit in the oven. I already have the pastry in the fridge. It's just about ready, so let's get the filling together." Tessa gestured to a container of cherries and a bowl on the counter. "I froze these when they were in season, and this is the perfect opportunity to use them. Fresh cherries always taste so much better than canned, and it's only a little more effort. I pitted them before freezing, but we have to cut them."

As they prepared the cherries, Cassie filled her in on her encounter with Chase.

"So, his theory is that Helen killed Lisbeth? Maybe Lisbeth was angry that she couldn't get the money out of the trust account for the riding school?" Tessa suggested.

"Even if she was, though, why would that lead to Helen wanting to kill her? That doesn't add up." Cassie added the cherries to the bowl.

"True, but we need to look into it more. You said Chase said Lisbeth didn't trust Helen. We need to put in a little lemon juice, some vanilla, almond extract, and salt. Oh, can you hand me that cornstarch, please?" Tessa pointed to a shelf above the counter. "I like the filling to be pretty thick, and sweet." She grabbed the sugar. "The lemon juice gives it just a bit of tartness, but that actually makes the sauce taste even sweeter. Then we just toss it all together." She smiled as she added the ingredients to the bowl. "A little bit of stirring and that's all it takes. When the pie cooks, it will become a delicious goo."

"Goo? Is that the technical cooking term?" Cassie grinned.

"Yes, yes it is." Tessa laughed as she rolled out some dough on a floured cutting board. "This part is the hardest part, but also the most rewarding. My lattice cherry pie is a work of art. We have to slice the top crust into even strips so we can crisscross them over the top of the pie. Here, you work on that, while I get the bottom crusts ready."

"Me?" Cassie took the knife Tessa handed her. "What if I do it wrong?"

"There's no way to do it wrong, just do your best." After a few minutes of stirring and slicing, Tessa admired Cassie's work. "They look great. Let's get the cherry mixture in the crusts and we'll get to work on the art."

Once the pie shells were filled, the two worked together to drape the sliced pie crust across the top of each pie.

"Perfect." Tessa smiled as she took a step back and looked at the pies.

"A little off-balance, maybe?" Cassie wrinkled her nose as she nudged one of the pie strips with her finger.

"Everyone should be a little different. That's part of the artistry." Tessa winked at her, then slid the pies into the oven. "All right, while these bake, you and I need to make a plan."

"A plan? What kind of plan?"

"Tomorrow, we're going to speak to Kim and Jill, Helen, and Gordon, again. The pies will hopefully get us in, but our questions will hopefully help us find the murderer."

CHAPTER 14

The following morning, Cassie and Tessa headed to Jill and Kim's apartment. There hadn't been any major updates from Oliver and they were eager to get to the bottom of things.

"Okay, are we ready for this?" Tessa reached up and knocked on their apartment door before Cassie could answer.

Jill opened the door and raised her eyebrows. "You two again?"

"We brought you some comfort food." Cassie thrust the pie toward her. "Could we speak to you for just a few minutes, please?"

"Oh, wow. Thank you." Jill smiled as she took the pie and stepped out of the way to let them through. "Okay. Any chance you have any new news about Drake?"

"No, sorry." Tessa led the way into the apartment.

"Richard's been calling us all night, begging for us to help him come up with the money for the ransom." Jill carried the pie to the kitchen. She passed by Kim who paced back and forth in front of the couch.

"We don't have anything to offer him." Kim turned toward them and crossed her arms. "Of course, if we had it, we would offer to help. But just like them, we can't access our trust money that easily."

"The worst part is that Lisbeth didn't deserve any of this. All she wanted to do was take care of the ranch." Jill clasped her hands together. "She loved those horses so much."

"And all her brothers did was give her trouble," Kim huffed as she dropped down onto the couch. "The two of them never let her rest."

"I know that Richard has a history of some bad financial decisions, but what did Drake do?" Cassie sat down beside her.

"He also gave her trouble, but in a different way. He's studying business management, but he always had these great new business ideas, including what to do with the ranch. At one point, he even wanted to turn it into a golf course. Can you believe that?" Kim let out a short laugh. "Our grandfather would have been furious."

"So, he had a lot of big ideas. And none of them worked out well?" Tessa looked between them.

"Yes, they all failed, most before they even started. But it was worse than that. He'd make promises to people and then spring it on Richard and Lisbeth. Of course, they wouldn't want anything to do with it, and it would turn into a big argument. We weren't close, after the will was read. But when I did happen to see Lisbeth in town, or notice one of her posts, I could tell how strained she was." Kim closed her eyes for a moment.

"So, you used to be close?" Cassie asked.

"Very. We always rode the horses together, ever since we were kids." Jill held her hand low, as if measuring the height of a child. "But Lisbeth did get fed up at times. I think she was tired of always being the one taking care of everyone."

"I still can't believe she cut us out like that." Kim sighed.

"I tried to talk to her a few days ago and she just

ignored me. I mean, what I had to say was important," Jill said.

"What did you want to talk to her about?" Cassie asked.

"There was money missing from the family funds. I'd crunched the numbers and found the inconsistencies, so Helen started looking into it." Jill glanced at Kim. "She said there would be an investigation into the discrepancies and that it would all get sorted out. But I wasn't sure if Helen had told Lisbeth about it, and I wanted to make sure she knew what was happening. I left Lisbeth a message explaining it all, but I have no idea if she ever listened to it. I thought if we joined forces we could help work out what had happened with the money."

"I don't know why you bothered to even try to speak to her about it." A bitterness entered Kim's voice. "She obviously didn't want anything to do with us. She didn't even offer to involve us in the riding school she was starting up."

"You knew about that?" Cassie looked at Kim.

"Yes. But she didn't want us to have anything to do with it, which was ridiculous. Jill and I love horses. We're teachers at the local high school, but our real passion is horses. It was on our family ranch. The whole thing is just very upsetting." Kim sighed. "Listen, I know you both have good intentions, and we appreciate the pie, but we're just trying to get through the day here. We just want to focus on getting Drake home."

"We understand. We'll let you know if we find out anything." Tessa opened the door for Cassie and led the way to the jeep.

"I know they say they care about Lisbeth, but there was also a lot of animosity there." Cassie opened the passenger side door and hopped in.

"I agree. I wonder if they teamed up with Richard to do this?" Tessa slid behind the wheel.

"Oh, I hadn't thought of that. That's very possible. They believe their grandfather was unfair to them and they were owed more. With Lisbeth gone, and Drake out of the picture, maybe it would leave them with a larger chunk to split with Richard."

"Or maybe they did it just to get access to the ransom money from the family trust." Tessa started the engine. "We need to look at them more, but right now I want to speak with Helen. She's been hiding some things, and I want the truth."

CHAPTER 15

"Hello, again." Tessa flashed a smile at the man behind the front desk in Helen's office. "Do you remember us?"

"Sure I do. But what is that amazing smell?" Allan sniffed the air.

"Cherry pie." Tessa held it out to him. "For you and Helen."

"Oh, yes, I'll take that." Allan grinned as he stood and took the pie from Tessa's hands. "Thank you."

"You're welcome. Does Helen have a moment to see us, please?" Tessa asked.

"Let me just check." Allan picked up the phone and spoke softly into it, before he pointed toward the inner office. "Sure, go ahead in."

"Thanks." Tessa strode over to Helen's office door. She gave a light knock, then opened the door.

"Come in," Helen called out from behind her desk and waved them in.

As Tessa and Cassie stepped inside, Cassie wanted to believe that Helen had nothing to do with what had happened. But knowing she was managing the funds for both sets of siblings, and appeared to be hiding some things, put her right in the middle of everything.

"Allan said you brought us a pie. Thank you." Helen smiled up at them, then gestured around her. "Sorry, things are a little cluttered. I'm supposed to meet with Richard, Jill, and Kim soon. We need to go over what's changed since Lisbeth's death."

"Already?" Tessa sat down in a chair in front of her desk. The desk had a few trays of small sandwiches.

"It's important to stay on top of everything." Helen leaned forward. "Also, Richard's hounding me for money for the ransom, and I'm trying to figure out how I can make that work. Their trust money is tied up in investments, and I can't access so much so quickly."

"Kim and Jill mentioned that there's money missing from the family account." Cassie eyed the sandwiches as her stomach rumbled. Aside from a few bites of a bagel before she ran out of the house that morning, she hadn't eaten anything else, and her body was letting her know.

"Did you tell the police?" Tessa asked.

"No, that's a family matter." Helen paused as if she might have heard the rumble, and gestured to the sandwiches. "Please, eat. I ordered these for the family, but there's more than enough, and I don't even know if they're going to want to eat them."

"Thank you." Cassie plucked one of the sandwiches from the tray.

"Whether it's a family matter or not, it might be relevant to solving a murder and kidnapping. The police need all the information they can get." Tessa squinted at Helen.

"Look, discretion is crucial." Helen clasped her hands together. "It's not my place to disclose anything. But now that Kim and Jill have brought it up, I can address it. I've only just realized the full extent of the issue. I thought everything was in order, but now I see that money has been missing for a while. I've already started looking into it."

"What do you suspect was happening? You must have some idea," Tessa said.

Helen let out a deep breath as she shook her

head. "I do have my suspicions." She hesitated, then continued, "Richard was always looking for ways to access the fund. I thought Lisbeth's extra restrictions had stopped him, but maybe there was more going on behind the scenes than I realized. I'll need to go over the records again." She glanced between them, her lips pressed into a thin line. "I hate to think of what this could mean. I'm already reviewing everything carefully."

"Did you know anything about Lisbeth getting money from her neighbor to start the riding school?" Tessa leaned forward.

"She took money from Gordon?" Helen narrowed her eyes. "No, I didn't know anything about that. Are you sure?"

"That's what Gordon claims. But we haven't seen any paperwork to support it. Didn't you see the money in her account?" Cassie finished her sandwich.

"I don't have access to Lisbeth's personal account. Just the family trust accounts. She asked me for money from the trust for the riding school, but when I said I doubt I would be able to help her, and she would have to go through the official channels for me to check, I didn't hear from her about it again." Helen sat back in her chair. "I don't think she wanted to go through the rigorous process, considering that I didn't think I would be able to access the funds for the project anyway. I'm pretty thorough with the kids when they want money over a certain amount. They have to submit a lot of paperwork to me indicating what they intend to use it for, and the steps they'll take to replenish it."

"That sounds like a lot of work on your part," Tessa said.

"It is, but their grandfather had strict stipulations in his will about the account." Helen shrugged. "That's why Lisbeth was so frustrated when Richard was misusing funds. She was following the rules, but he wasn't. And that's why she tightened access even further. Lisbeth and Richard fought over it constantly." Her jaw tightened. "Lisbeth showed me some texts from him. He was furious with her for telling me that I shouldn't allow him to withdraw any funds without her approval. He even tried to intimidate her."

"Richard didn't tell us anything about that." Cassie glanced at Tessa, then looked back at Helen.

"That doesn't surprise me. He probably didn't want you to know how much trouble he was causing." Helen sat back in her chair. "Look, the rules were outlined in Stuart's will, and it's my job to follow them."

"You followed the rules so well, but money's still missing." Cassie tilted her head to the side. "How could that happen?"

"That's what the investigation will determine. But it will take time." Helen's jaw tightened. "The more time I spend going over the same information, whether with you or the police, the less chance I have of finding a way to get the money for Drake's ransom." She gestured toward her office door. "I've already told you more than I normally would. Now, please, I have to get back to work."

"Okay." Cassie stood up and walked toward the door.

Tessa followed after but stopped in the doorway and looked back at Helen. "And where did you say you were yesterday morning, before sunrise?"

"At home, of course. Why?" Helen's voice took on a slightly higher pitch. "You can't possibly think I had anything to do with Lisbeth's death."

"Just covering all the bases." Tessa started through the door and Cassie followed her.

They passed by the receptionist who was already

eating a slice of pie. "Excellent, thank you so much!" Allan dabbed his lips with a napkin.

"You're welcome." Tessa led the way out of the office.

By the time they'd reached the jeep, Tessa was already on the phone with Oliver. She switched it to speaker as she climbed into the driver's seat.

"So, you're saying that Helen claims she saw the texts on Lisbeth's phone?" Oliver's tone hardened. "We haven't been able to recover her phone. It's missing. We can't trace it. I'm waiting for the records to come through."

"So, you think the killer took it? Or destroyed it? Maybe Richard wanted to hide those texts." Cassie climbed up into the jeep. "But even without her phone you should be able to see the texts on Richard's phone, right? And we know that he has it because he was using it to call Drake."

"Yes, I should be able to see the texts on his phone. I have a few things to tie up here, then I'll go over to the ranch and try to get a look at his phone."

"We'll meet you over there. He's more likely to be helpful with us there. He did trust us with the information about the ransom note." Tessa ended the call before Oliver could argue, then turned on the jeep and backed out of the parking space.

"So, if Richard was fighting with Lisbeth about money, then found out that she borrowed some from Gordon, I think there's a good chance that he went after his sister for that money. If he found out that she was trying to start a riding school, instead of helping him with his debts, after practically cutting him off from the family funds, that might have been enough to push him over the edge." Cassie gripped her notebook tight as Tessa took a hard turn. "Tessa, slow down, we have to wait for Ollie to get there, and he said he had a few things to finish up. He won't be happy if we talk to Richard first."

"Sorry, I'm just a little distracted. I think Helen knows more about the missing money than she's letting on."

"You may be right. She may be using her supposed dedication to her clients' privacy to keep someone's secret. Maybe she helped Richard access the money?" Cassie suggested.

"That's possible." Tessa turned down the long drive that led to the Woodcrest ranch. "It looks like the officers are gone. I'm guessing Ollie pulled the police presence to make the kidnapper feel more comfortable and maybe slip up."

"Hopefully, it works," Cassie said.

"And hopefully, Richard's phone will give us some insight."

CHAPTER 16

Cassie peered through the windshield as they pulled up outside the ranch house. She noticed a green van in the driveway, the Little Leaf Creek vet logo gleaming on the side. A tall, slender woman, who looked about thirty, stood beside it. Her long, black hair was tied back in a ponytail, and she wore a neatly pressed button-up shirt and jeans.

"Looks like Dr. Harper's here." Tessa parked beside Drake's red pickup truck. "She gave Harry and the goats their shots this week. She was great with them, really patient, though she did say Billy and Gerry are the naughtiest goats she's ever met."

"That doesn't surprise me." Cassie laughed.

Cassie and Tessa hopped out of the jeep and headed toward the van.

"Dr. Harper," Tessa called out.

The woman turned toward them. "Tessa, I told you to call me Lynn." Her English accent was distinct.

"Sorry, Lynn." Tessa gestured toward Cassie. "This is Cassie."

Cassie noticed that Lynn's green eyes matched her grandfather's as she focused on her.

"I recognize you," Lynn said.

"I work at the diner. Mirabel's. I think I served you a few days ago." Cassie smiled.

"Oh, of course. Yes." Lynn finished securing her medical bag and shut the van door before turning back to them. "I was just double-checking on Phantom after his little adventure yesterday morning."

"Is he okay?" Tessa asked.

"He's fine." Lynn nodded reassuringly.

"Good to hear." Tessa smiled.

"It's been a rough couple of days." Lynn's shoulders stiffened. "I only met Lisbeth briefly, but I know how much this ranch meant to her. It's just awful."

"Your grandfather mentioned that you were going to be involved with the riding school," Tessa said.

"Yes, that was part of the reason I moved here." Lynn tucked a loose strand of hair behind her ear. "I didn't expect to leave London, but my relationship ended, and this felt like a fresh start." She cleared her throat. "I thought I'd help out at my grandfather's practice, and gradually take it over, and being the vet for the riding school was part of that."

"But now, it's not going ahead?" Cassie thought about how she never expected to move to Little Leaf Creek, but ended up there when she needed a fresh start herself.

Lynn glanced away for a moment before refocusing on them. "No, it won't."

"Do you know much about the family? About Richard and Drake?" Tessa asked.

"Not much, really." Lynn shifted her weight. "I met Drake a few days ago, when he came into the clinic to pick up some medication for one of the horses, and I only met Richard for the first time today."

"Here?" Cassie gestured around her.

"Yes, just about ten minutes ago." Lynn hesitated slightly, then lowered her voice. "I barely spoke to him. He got a phone call while I was here. He seemed really upset, angry, actually. I didn't catch much, but he kept talking about money."

"Could it have been about the ransom?" Cassie asked.

"Maybe." Lynn glanced toward the house. "I really don't know. He didn't say anything specific, but he was definitely worked up."

"All of this has him very upset," Tessa agreed. "Which is understandable, of course."

"Exactly." Lynn climbed into the driver's seat. "I'd better get to my next appointment. This was just a quick visit." She closed the door.

Cassie watched as the van pulled away, then turned to Tessa. "She must be on edge by all of this. To make such a big move after a heartbreak and practically walk right into this."

"Yes, it must have been a shock —" Tessa's words were cut off as the sudden roar of an engine broke through the quiet, and both of them turned toward the noise.

Oliver's police car rumbled down the dirt driveway toward the house, kicking up clouds of dust.

"There's Ollie." Tessa waited to greet him.

"Ladies." Oliver gave them a brief nod as he strode toward the house and onto the porch.

Tessa and Cassie followed from a distance as he approached the front door and knocked on it.

"Richard, it's Detective Oliver Graham. Can you come out here, please?"

The door swung open. Richard stepped out with wide, anxious eyes. "Did you find him? Please tell me he's okay!"

"No, I haven't found him, yet." Oliver met his eyes. "I'm here because I wanted to have a look at your phone, please."

"What?" Richard blinked. "Why?"

"Because I want to try and get to the bottom of this," Oliver said.

"Sure, right, anything to help." Richard pulled his phone out of his pocket and handed it over. "But this is such a waste of time. We need to concentrate on getting the ransom money together to get my brother back. Why are you wasting time on my phone?"

Oliver searched through the phone.

"Where are your text exchanges with Lisbeth, Richard?" Oliver looked up at him. "It looks like they've been deleted."

Cassie held in a gasp as she watched the tense interaction between the two.

"It's pretty suspicious that your sister's killed, and then your texts between each other are deleted." Oliver narrowed his eyes.

"What do you think were in those texts, anyway?" Richard asked.

"I heard that you and Lisbeth had been arguing about money and there are texts to prove it. It's time to tell the truth." Oliver squared his shoulders.

"If you really want to save your brother, you need to give Oliver all the details," Tessa spoke up.

"Okay, yes. We'd been fighting about money when Lisbeth completely cut me off from the family account. But I ended up in a desperate situation, and she didn't leave me hanging. She loaned some money to me. And our last few texts were about her needing the money back. I deleted the exchange when I found out she was dead. They were just too upsetting to read. I know I said I would repay it quickly, but things didn't go to plan. I needed it to cover some serious debts, so, of course, I used it for that. I didn't have anything to give her, yet. She said it wasn't her money and the person wanted it back. That she never should have given it to me but she wanted to help me. I didn't have it. What could I do?" Richard looked between each of them in turn, as he pleaded for understanding. He took a sharp breath. "Oh, no. Is that why someone killed her? Because I couldn't repay her?"

"Did she tell you where she got the money?" Cassie asked.

"No, I don't know where she got it. I was just happy that she gave it to me." Richard shook his head.

Cassie's heart dropped as she witnessed the grief and guilt cloud his eyes.

"That's why they took Drake? They still want their money back?" Richard clenched his hands into fists. "I never meant to put anyone in danger."

"We know you didn't. And we also don't know if that's the motivation behind all of this. We're here to help you. But you need to tell us the whole story." Tessa crossed her arms. "Did you see her the night before she died? I felt like you were hiding something about that night."

Richard hesitated for a moment before answering. "Yes. When she came home the night before she was killed, she asked me for the money again. When I told her I still didn't have it, she said she didn't know what she was going to do. It wasn't hers to give away like that. Then she got a phone call, so I went to my room. I was going to try and do what I could to help her. That was it, I swear. I never hurt her."

"And you didn't tell me because you knew it would make you look more suspicious. Which it absolutely does." Oliver narrowed his eyes.

"Please don't arrest me." Richard looked at Oliver. "At least not until after the ransom drop. Please, I just want to get my little brother home."

"That's what I want, too." Oliver's tone softened slightly. "But unless you're willing to tell me the whole truth, that's going to be hard to accomplish."

"That's the whole truth. She gave me some money and needed it back. I had no idea it could lead to this." Richard's shoulders slumped.

As Oliver and Richard continued discussing the details of his argument with his sister, Cassie met Tessa's eyes. She stepped closer to her and spoke softly. "We know where she probably got that money from, don't we?"

"Maybe we do," Tessa agreed. "Let's go find out."

"Should we tell Ollie what we're doing?" Cassie

glanced back over her shoulder at Oliver and Richard.

"He has enough on his plate right now. We know that she received some money from Gordon. So, that's where we should start." Tessa led the way back to the jeep.

CHAPTER 17

"What's Gordon going to tell us that he didn't tell us last time?" Cassie peered through the windshield as Tessa turned down the long driveway that led to Gordon's house. "I feel like he's holding out on us, but how are we going to get him to tell us more?"

"I'm hoping this pie will butter him up enough to get him talking." Tessa pointed over her shoulder at the pie in the back seat. "It's worth a shot, right?"

"Right." Cassie looked over Gordon's property as they approached his house. "I can't even imagine why a man with this much wealth would murder someone over a small investment. And the kidnapping is risky. He might never get the money. It just doesn't make sense."

"No, it doesn't. But people don't always act rationally." Tessa parked in front of the house. "The important thing is to keep an open mind and consider him a possible suspect, no matter how things appear. Maybe Lisbeth owed money to someone else, or maybe she needed it back from Richard for a completely different reason, but we have to investigate all avenues."

"That's possible. If she didn't take it out of the family fund, and none of her siblings or cousins had money to give, who else would she have borrowed money from?"

"Good question. From what we know, it's not like she had many options. Unless, maybe there's someone in her life that we're overlooking." Tessa stepped out of the jeep. "Let's start by seeing if we can eliminate Gordon as a suspect. He claims he has an alibi, but the majority of that time was spent driving from here to a commercial shoot. Which means that he could be lying, and as far as I know, Ollie hasn't been able to verify his presence at the shoot, yet, either."

Cassie glanced over at a shed in the corner of the yard and noticed someone standing beside it.

Tessa followed her line of sight.

"Frank." Tessa started toward the man who

looked to be in his late fifties. He was wearing faded jeans and a T-shirt.

"Tessa, Cassie." Frank tipped his baseball cap toward them.

"You work for Gordon?" Tessa kept her tone casual as Cassie stepped up beside her.

"Have for years." Frank leaned back against the shed wall.

"Did you hear what happened at the Woodcrests?" Tessa pointed in the direction of the ranch.

"Yes. Everyone has, haven't they?" A faint smile crossed his lips before it disappeared. "And I had nothing to do with it. No one's going to pin this on me this time."

"This time?" Cassie asked.

"As you know, Tessa, Stuart accused me of being involved in Danny's kidnapping all those years ago." Frank waved his hand through the air. "Thought I was involved with the drifters who took him, but I had nothing to do with any of it. Lost a lot of work because of those false accusations."

"I remember that. Do you know Lisbeth and her brothers?" Tessa asked.

"Only when they were kids. After the whole

thing, I couldn't stay far enough away from the place." Frank glanced toward the ranch.

"So, you have no idea who's responsible for this?" Tessa studied him.

"None." Frank shook his head.

"Where were you early yesterday morning?" Tessa tried to keep her tone casual.

"You think I had something to do with this? Are you crazy?" Frank scoffed, then turned and walked into the shed.

Cassie followed Tessa back toward the house.

"Well, that is interesting." Cassie glanced at Tessa and spoke softly. "He avoided your question about where he was."

"He did, and Frank was absolutely livid when he was accused by Stuart. I never thought he had anything to do with it, but who knows."

"So, you think he could have done this?" Cassie asked.

"I'm not sure. He doesn't have any criminal history that I know about, but he has a temper, and he was furious with Stuart. Maybe he thought it was time to take some revenge?"

"We should ask Gordon about him," Cassie said.

"Absolutely." Tessa led the way to Gordon's door and knocked.

The door opened a few inches. "Yes? What is it?" Gordon's voice sounded strained.

"Gordon, can we speak with you for a few minutes, please?" Cassie asked.

"Okay, but you have to make it quick." Gordon opened the door and gestured for them to enter his very dimly lit home.

"We brought you a homemade cherry pie." Cassie held it out to him.

"Thank you." Gordon pointed to a table by the entrance. "You can just put it there."

Cassie placed it on the table and continued into the house. She was surprised he'd just left it there, and hadn't taken it into the kitchen or asked her to. But the whole situation seemed strange.

"You said you'd recently given Lisbeth some capital to start her riding school. That's right, isn't it?" Tessa made her way through the front hallway into the even darker living room, where Gordon had settled in a chair.

"Yes. I thought it was a good investment. Obviously, her brothers weren't doing anything to help her with that. I'd known her grandfather before he passed away, and I knew he would have wanted her to be successful, so I offered to help. I mean, it was an investment, of course. I expected to receive the money back, and more, once she'd opened the school. But I knew that would take a little time." Gordon leaned his head back against the chair.

"When did you give her the money?" Cassie strained to see his face through the darkness. It was hard to tell if he was lying without being able to see his features. She wondered if that might be the reason for the dim lighting.

"About a month ago." Gordon's eyes narrowed. "Why? Did something happen to my money? I know this is a delicate time, but I do expect to receive it back."

"We don't know. We just wanted to find out more about what was happening with her finances." Cassie pulled her notebook out of her pocket, though she couldn't see it well enough to write in it. "Could we turn a light on? It's pretty dark in here."

Tessa reached for the light switch on the wall.

"No, don't!" Gordon gasped. "I'm sorry, I have such a terrible migraine, and I'm sensitive to the light. Everything that's happening has me so stressed out, I just can't get rid of the headache."

Cassie gave Tessa a slight nod.

"Maybe we should come back another time?"

Cassie backed up toward the hallway. "If you think of anything, please reach out."

Tessa turned back to face him. "Sorry, just one quick question before we go. We just saw Frank. Do you know him well?"

"He's been working for me for years." Gordon nodded, then winced as he touched his head.

"Does he ever talk about the Woodcrests and what happened with Danny all those years ago?" Tessa asked.

"I'm sorry, but can we please do this another time? I just need to rest." Gordon let out a deep breath.

Tessa steered Cassie toward the door. "Of course. I hope you feel better soon. If you think of anything, let us know."

As Cassie stepped outside, she blinked against the sunlight, then followed Tessa toward the jeep. "Well, he was in a hurry to get rid of us."

"Migraines can be rough." Tessa looked back at the house as she opened the jeep door.

"I'm sure they can, but I wish he'd been able to answer more of our questions. I wanted to ask him about Chase and if he thought he could be involved." Cassie sat down in the passenger seat.

"Well, if we have questions about Chase, maybe

we should just go ask him directly." Tessa climbed into the driver's seat.

"The question is, will we be able to find him?" Cassie recalled seeing him at the diner yesterday. "He didn't seem to have a problem being out with his girlfriend, right after his boss had been killed."

"He lives in a trailer on the ranch. Even if he's not home, maybe we can get a look inside to see what he might have been up to recently. He may be trying to hide something." Tessa turned down the long driveway to the ranch.

CHAPTER 18

"After everything Lisbeth did for Chase, do you really think he would kill her? And why?" Cassie glanced over at Tessa as she drove down the ranch's driveway. "I find it hard to believe."

"We can't dismiss the possibility just yet. He's got a record for a few fights, which shows he's got a temper, but they weren't especially violent. Still, prison can change people. It can make them more volatile, especially without support after release." Tessa winced. "So, while Lisbeth might have been willing to take a chance on him, that doesn't necessarily mean that she made the right decision." Her voice trailed off. "And it doesn't look like we'll have to hunt him down. Isn't that him by the barn?" She parked and turned the engine off.

"Yes, it is." Cassie stepped out of the jeep, then noticed Chase was staring at the barn. Fixated. "Maybe this has just caught up to him."

"Maybe. He was close with Lisbeth. She gave him a chance when no one else would. I'm sure this must be hard for him." Tessa cleared her throat, hoping the sound would draw his attention.

Chase continued to stand perfectly still outside the barn, staring at it.

"Chase," Cassie called out to him as she approached. "What are you doing?"

"Oh, sorry." Chase turned to face her. "I was trying to work out what to do next. I usually have a routine I follow, but not having access to the barn is just throwing everything off. And then, of course, Lisbeth is dead, so I don't know what she would want me to do." He wiped a hand across his face. "I guess I'm just feeling a little lost."

"That's understandable." Tessa joined them. "But you'll have to keep out of the barn for now, until the police release it."

"I know. The horses are out in the paddock at the moment, and I'm using the old barn." Chase pointed in that direction. "It's a bit cramped, but it'll do."

"You must care about them a lot." Cassie studied his expression. "How long have you been working here?"

"Only a few months. But it feels like forever. I thought I'd finally found a good place for me. Now, I have no idea what's going to happen. I have no idea what I'm going to do." Chase sighed. "It's not surprising, I guess. This has been the pattern that's played out throughout my life. I just thought I could finally change it."

"It sounds like Lisbeth had a lot of faith in you." Cassie settled her eyes on his.

"Yes." Chase curled his hands into fists briefly. "Most people don't look past a criminal record, but Lisbeth did."

"Was it only that?" Tessa studied him. "Or was it more than that? Was there something going on between the two of you?"

"What?" Chase blinked. "Of course not. It was just business."

"Did she tell you about the riding school she'd planned to start?" Tessa searched his eyes.

"Yeah, I know about the riding school." Chase

rested his hands on his hips. "That's why she hired me. She wanted me to help with the horses, so she could keep focused on starting the school."

"Were you worried that eventually Richard would win out and she would get rid of you?" Cassie watched the way he shifted from foot to foot and didn't seem to know what to do with his hands.

"A little. I mean, I love the ranch. From the moment I set foot on it, I knew it was where I belonged. So, I was excited to be part of everything. But I knew that Richard didn't want me here, and he was always buzzing in Lisbeth's ear about hiring me." Chase rolled his eyes. "He didn't want me on the ranch due to my record. It was quite a while ago and nothing serious. She told him to back off, but I was worried he was wearing her down."

"What about Drake? You two are pretty close in age. Are you good friends?" Cassie asked.

"Friends with Drake?" Chase chuckled. "Not a chance. Drake sees me as the help, nothing else. I don't think we've exchanged more than a few words since I started working here. But Lisbeth thought the world of him. She was always talking about his ideas like they would amount to something. I listened. I let her believe in him, but I know a con man when I see one. He was just as bad as Richard, always trying to get money from her. I tried it myself, thinking she was an easy mark. But she didn't budge an inch with me. She was only a pushover with her siblings."

"Have you ever seen their cousins, Jill and Kim, around the ranch?" Tessa asked.

"Sure." A faint smile crossed Chase's lips. "They come around. They like to ride the horses."

"They come around often?" Cassie tried to keep the suspicion out of her voice. She recalled the hay on Kim's sweater and realized that this might explain it.

"Yes, once or twice a week," Chase said.

"Wait, but I thought they weren't allowed on the ranch?" Tessa's words drew a hardened expression from him. "Richard mentioned something about Lisbeth banning them after they had an argument about ownership. They even said they aren't allowed here."

"Look, they grew up on the ranch, too. It's a huge job to exercise the horses myself. So, when they showed up one day when it was just me, and they asked to ride, I let them. And then they told me the whole story about how the ranch was stolen from them, and so I told them I'd let them know whenever Lisbeth and her brothers weren't around, so they could come out and ride the horses. What harm could it do?" Chase waved his hand dismissively.

"Sure, and it made your job easier?" Tessa said.

"Yes, it did." Chase shrugged as he looked straight at her. "Win-win, right?"

"Right, unless Lisbeth got wind of what was happening and that led to an argument with Kim and Jill that led to Lisbeth's death." Tessa frowned. "This is something you definitely should have told the police about."

"No one asked." Chase furrowed his brow. "I know better than to volunteer information to the police. Besides, I didn't hurt Lisbeth, and I really don't think Kim or Jill would have hurt her. They were very nice to me, especially Kim." He paused for a moment. "If I wasn't with Mallory, I definitely would have asked her out. Look, like I said, they had nothing to do with this."

Tessa glanced at her phone as it beeped with a text. "If you think of anything that might be important, let us know, please."

"Sure." Chase started to walk away.

Tessa's eyes widened as she read over the text. "That's interesting."

"What?" Cassie asked.

"Mark just found out that Danny, the ranch hand who was kidnapped, has a brother, Rhett, who's been staying with their father, Norman, in Rombsby for a few days." Tessa looked up at her. "The timing seems too coincidental, doesn't it?"

"It does. Looks like we just got a new suspect."

CHAPTER 19

Cassie and Tessa headed straight to Norman's house.

Cassie matched Tessa's pace up the narrow driveway toward a modest home that appeared well-kept. The lawn was neat, and the house had a fresh coat of paint.

Tessa was eager to speak to Rhett as soon as possible. Even though the ransom drop was happening very soon, she knew they couldn't rely on it going smoothly and the kidnapper being caught.

Tessa knocked on the wooden door. A few moments later, it swung open, revealing a man about forty with sharp blue eyes.

Tessa's breath caught as she stared at him in disbelief. She hadn't expected to see him here, but even after twenty years, there was no mistaking him. "Danny?"

"Who's asking?" Danny tightened his grip on the doorframe.

"I'm Tessa and this is Cassie." She gestured to Cassie.

"Tessa." Danny squinted at her. "The detective?"

Tessa hesitated for a moment, shocked that he would remember her. "That's right. Retired now. I haven't seen you for so long. I'm surprised you remember me."

"I could never forget you. After everything I went through, you were so kind to me when I was released." A genuine warmth filled Danny's eyes.

"I'm just glad I could help." Tessa smiled. "Have you got a minute?"

"Sure. Come in." Danny stepped inside and they followed him.

As Cassie and Tessa walked into the living room, which was cozy but simple with worn furniture and family photos on the walls, they saw a woman who looked a few years younger than Danny sitting on the carpet beside a toddler, as he moved a small toy car back and forth.

"Tessa and Cassie. This is my wife, Patty, and my son, Jet." Danny gestured to them.

"Nice to meet you." Patty smiled and met her husband's eyes for a moment. "I was just about to put Jet down for a nap." She stood, then scooped her son up, and headed down the hallway.

"I guess you're here because of what happened at the Woodcrest ranch?" Danny gestured to a couch for them, and he took a seat in a chair facing it. "Rhett just called to tell me about it."

"Yes, we're trying to figure out what happened there." Tessa sat down beside Cassie.

"Well, I had nothing to do with any of it." Danny held up his hands. "I just can't believe I walked into this mess. I'm surprised the police haven't been out to see me, yet. I mean they're going to suspect me for sure. That's why you're here, isn't it? I never should have come back here."

"Why did you?" Tessa leaned forward.

"My wife and I recently had another baby, a daughter, and I wanted my family to meet her. So, Rhett and I arranged to come here with our families to visit Dad." Danny cleared his throat. "It's been so long since my kidnapping, and I wanted to try and put it all behind me. Especially seeing as I've got a family now, I thought I should move on."

"Congratulations!" Tessa smiled.

"Thank you," Danny said, the pride evident in

his tone. "I would introduce you to Daisy, but she's sleeping."

"Maybe another time." Tessa met his eyes. "It does seem like an amazing coincidence that you're back here and there's been another kidnapping at the ranch."

"That's all it is. A coincidence." Danny's shoulders slumped. "And I have no doubt I'll have the police on my back soon. I think I'll leave before that happens."

"You shouldn't run." Tessa held up her hands. "You'll just look guilty."

"I know," Danny conceded. "But I feel like I don't have a choice."

"Where were you early yesterday morning, before sunrise? If you have an alibi you won't have to worry about any of this," Tessa said.

"You really think I had something to do with this?" Danny asked.

"No." Tessa tried to sound convincing, but she had her doubts. "But someone might want people to think you did."

"I hadn't even thought of that." Danny swallowed hard. "I was at home sleeping."

"Who knew you were back in the area?" Tessa pressed. "Did you tell anyone ahead of time? Did anyone that knew you when you lived here before, find out you were back?"

"My family, of course, and I had dinner at a new restaurant in Lockersby a couple of nights ago, and I saw Gordon, the Woodcrests' neighbor there. But what could that have to do with anything?" Danny squinted at them.

Cassie and Tessa exchanged a quick glance.

"Did you speak to him?" Tessa focused back on Danny.

"Yes." Danny nodded. "He recognized me from when I worked on the ranch. He was surprised to see me. Asked what I was doing back in the area, how long I was staying, that kind of thing. He seemed a bit standoffish, as if he was asking the questions because he was expected to, not because he cared. But I figured that was Gordon being Gordon. Like I said, I had nothing to do with any of this."

"Do you have any idea who might have?" Cassie asked.

"No, none. I haven't had any connection to the Woodcrests since I left town." Danny shook his head. "I just never should have come back here."

"If you're innocent, then you have nothing to

worry about," Tessa reassured him. "The detective on the case is very good."

"I hope you're right," Danny said.

"And if you think of anything, give me a call." Tessa stood up and handed him a card with her number on.

"Okay." Danny took it from her and started toward the door.

"It was good to see you again." Tessa and Cassie followed him.

"And you." Danny held the door open for them.

Cassie and Tessa stepped out and walked down the driveway.

When Danny had closed the door, Cassie glanced over at Tessa. "He seemed to think very highly of you."

"He did." Tessa tipped her head from side to side. "But maybe he was just trying to butter me up because he knows Ollie's on the case and he found out I'm close to him. Maybe he wants me on his side."

"I never thought of that. So, do you think he's involved?" Cassie turned toward her as they reached the jeep.

"I hate to think it, but it's possible. He held resentment toward the family. He's in town after so many years and this happens. He's clearly still angry."

"True." Cassie walked around to the passenger side. "What do you think about what he said about Gordon knowing he was here?"

"I'm not sure what to think, to be honest. We'll have to ask Gordon about it. But let's see if we can get an update from Ollie about the ransom drop first. I thought he would have texted by now." Tessa climbed into the jeep. "I'd hoped Drake would already have been released."

A knot formed in Cassie's stomach as she wondered if something had gone wrong at the ransom drop. She hoped that Drake was okay.

CHAPTER 20

Cassie and Tessa walked into the bustling police station. After an officer made sure that Oliver was free to see them, they headed toward his office.

As soon as Oliver looked up, Tessa knew things hadn't gone to plan. The frown on his face gave him away immediately.

"I guess you want an update?" Oliver clasped his hands together.

"Yes, absolutely." Cassie's voice raised in anticipation.

"Well, Richard got the ransom money from Helen and we went to the drop." Oliver's voice was edged with frustration. "But Richard chickened out and refused to leave the money."

"What?" Tessa gasped.

"The plan was for him to leave the money on a bench at the park as arranged. We would have caught the kidnapper, when they picked it up." Oliver frowned. "But instead, Richard sat down on the bench for a while, then he ran back to me with the money, where I was watching from the bushes. He said it was because he was worried that they would run off with the money and kill Drake."

"Do you think he botched the drop because he was involved?" Tessa suggested. "Maybe he really did kidnap Drake, or maybe he staged it with Drake and didn't have time to notify him to pick it up, or Drake couldn't get there for some reason. Richard couldn't just wait and risk some stranger finding it, and he also couldn't admit that no one was coming to get it, because he's the kidnapper. This way, the money's still in play."

"Maybe. But what if he's telling the truth? He's right. Once the kidnapper has the money, there's no reason to keep Drake alive. What if he really is trying to protect his little brother?" Oliver frowned. "If that's the case, we have to assume the kidnapper's been tipped off about the police. But at this point, it seems as if the whole town knows about the kidnapping, so I'm sure the kidnapper expects that the police are involved. We're waiting now, hoping they'll organize another drop."

"We have something to tell you." Tessa explained how Danny was in town, and Gordon knew he was here.

"Danny's really here?" Oliver's voice raised slightly. "I'll go talk to him right now."

"Just take it easy on him." Tessa held up her hands. "I could be wrong, but I don't think he did this, and this has to be bringing up all of the memories of what happened to him."

"Okay." Oliver clearly still respected Tessa's opinion.

"Is there anything else you can tell us before you head off?" Tessa asked.

"Not much. We still haven't been able to find Lisbeth's phone, but we were able to access her phone records, which show her recent calls and texts."

"Anything interesting?" Tessa glanced at the papers on his desk.

"Not really. Just the calls you would expect to the farm supply store, vet, Helen, things like that." Oliver grabbed a file from his desk. "Of course, there were the texts between Richard and her that he told us about, and she'd also received quite a few calls from Gordon."

"We'll see if we can find out anything else." Tessa glanced at Cassie. "I need to check on Harry and the goats first, though."

"Okay." Cassie stood up.

"Let me know if you come across anything." Oliver walked them out of the office and toward the doors of the police station. "But use caution."

"We'll be careful." Tessa turned toward him. "You should pace yourself. I know you're not going to rest until Drake's safe, but you've just entered a marathon. This is no longer a sprint. Make sure you're keeping your head clear and your body nourished."

"Yes, Tessa." A faint smile tugged at the corners of Oliver's lips as he held her eyes for a moment before he turned and walked away.

Briefly, Cassie caught a glimpse of what life must have been like between Tessa and a teenage Oliver. She'd helped his mother, Alice, raise him until she'd passed away far too young, and then she became a mentor to him in the police force. Their dynamic was generally guarded and often tense, but there were moments when she witnessed the familial bond between them, and she found it fascinating.

"He'll be okay, Tessa. Mirabel will make sure he eats." Cassie smiled as she led the way to the jeep.

"Trust me, I've been much calmer ever since Mirabel and Ollie got together." Tessa settled in the driver's seat. "She does keep a good eye on him."

After a short drive, they turned onto their street. Tessa parked in her driveway and stepped down out of the jeep. "Give me a few minutes to tend to the pets, then we can head out."

"Okay, Sebastian's truck's here, so he should be inside. I just want to quicky touch base with him," Cassie said.

A high-pitched bleat from Gerry piercing the air drew Cassie's attention to the goats as they clamored near the gate in excitement to greet Tessa.

Cassie turned to find Sebastian walk up beside her.

"It's so good to see you." She opened her arms and Sebastian hugged her. She immediately felt a sense of comfort.

"And you." Sebastian's brown eyes lit up as he smiled. "How are you?"

"Okay. But I just really want this all solved," Cassie said.

"It will be." Sebastian looked at the goats as they demanded their attention. "I think the boys need some treats."

"Yes, I think they do." Cassie reached her hands out to the goats to greet them. She'd never really had a pet herself, but since moving in next to Tessa, she felt as if she shared the joy and chaos of her two goats and loyal collie. She reached into her pocket, pulled out a bag of carrot pieces, and threw a few to the goats.

"Well, I've fed Harry." Tessa descended the porch. "And Mark sent me a text. He's found out more about the Woodcrests and the family trust, so I want to go and find out what."

"Okay great, you go see him, then you can fill me in." Cassie smiled.

"Do you want to come with?" Tessa asked.

"No, that's okay. I want to spend some time with Sebastian. We can do a little research. And you and Mark can have some time alone."

"I don't need to be alone with Mark," Tessa huffed.

"I know." Cassie held back a laugh at Tessa's defensiveness. "But it can't do any harm, and I would like to spend some time with Sebastian."

Tessa glanced past her at Sebastian who was

busying himself petting the goats, then looked back at her.

"Okay, I'll check in with you as soon as I know anything new." Tessa returned to her jeep as Cassie and Sebastian headed into their house.

CHAPTER 21

On the drive to Mark's office, Tessa thought about her relationship with him. Her connection with Oliver's mother had been the closest she'd felt in her life, at least until she'd met Cassie, and being a big part of raising Oliver had meant the world to her. When she'd tried to shut the world out it was the loneliest time she'd ever experienced, and she had to admit that finding a romantic connection with Mark, after decades of the single life, left her quite flustered.

Tessa stepped out of the jeep and headed straight for Mark's office. They'd worked together for many years as she leaned on him for his legal advice and his less-than legal connections when she was working as a police officer. They had a long history, and she enjoyed his company.

Tessa's heart raced as she opened the door and stepped inside the empty reception area. She tried to steady her heartbeat and refused to acknowledge the excitement she felt at the thought of seeing him.

As Tessa stepped into the doorway of Mark's inner office he looked up at her with a warm smile, then he walked over in his bright purple suit and green shoes and hugged her.

He pulled back and looked past her into the main area of the office. "Just you?"

"Yes, just me." Tessa settled into a chair in front of his desk. "So, what have you found out?"

"Helen wasn't the only lawyer hired by the family." Mark sat down behind his desk and looked across it at her.

"What do you mean?"

"Kim and Jill hired an estate lawyer to contest the will over their loss of the ranch. But they recently let him go." Mark sat back in his chair.

"That's odd. Why would they hire him just to fire him? Was he unable to find a way to appeal?" Tessa asked.

"He said he'd found a few options. He wasn't sure if they would win, but he told them he felt it was worth trying. However, shortly after he'd filed the suit, they backed out and withdrew it."

"Really? So, why do you think they dropped the lawsuit?" Tessa narrowed her eyes.

"Maybe they changed their minds and they didn't want the hassle of a legal battle," Mark suggested.

"Or maybe they came up with a better plan?" Tessa snapped her fingers. "Maybe they knew that they were going to kill Lisbeth, and they planned to get rid of Drake, but needed some money quickly, so they held him for ransom first. Maybe they even planned to take Richard out next. They'll inherit everything if all their cousins are dead, won't they?"

"Possibly. I'd have to check the will over again to be certain."

"Okay, let's do that." Tessa glanced at the clock on the wall. "Unless you have somewhere else you need to be?"

"Only right here with you." Mark grinned, then picked up a folder from his desk. "Let's dig in." He started reading through the document. "Wait a minute." He squinted at the papers. "This doesn't make any sense."

"What do you mean?" Tessa rounded the desk

and looked over his shoulder to peer at the paper he held. "Tell me what I'm looking at."

"See this?" Mark pointed at the paper. "This whole list of stipulations that have to be met in order for the beneficiaries to access the funds, it's clearly been added in after the fact."

"What does that mean?"

"Here, let me show you." Mark caught her hand and guided it to a certain point in the text. "The font, both type and size change here. It's like someone cut and pasted this whole list into an original document. And, if I can get to the original file, I can almost guarantee that this was added in after it was created."

"Which means someone else altered the will?" Tessa fixed her gaze on the text. "But why would they want to add all these restrictions on withdrawing money? It limited their chances of being successful."

"I have a theory." Mark sat back in his chair.

"What?" Tessa's voice raised in anticipation.

"I don't think it was any of the grandkids. I think someone else benefited from making those changes."

"Who?"

"Helen's the one who stood to make money

every time one of her clients consulted her about withdrawing funds from the account. She's the one who gained more control by adding these rules." Mark's eyes widened. "I know it sounds ridiculous, but I think she might have been the one to put them there to retain some kind of control over the estate."

"Yes, you're right. It does make sense that she's the one who added the requirements. But I don't think this is about control." Tessa's jaw tightened as the pieces began to fall into place. "I think it's about much more than that."

"Tell me." Mark met her gaze.

"I think it's about theft." Tessa arched an eyebrow. "Helen keeps pointing to Richard, but she's the one who controlled the accounts. If there were so many restrictions, how did the money keep vanishing? Either she was asleep at the wheel, or she was the one stealing the money. Richard was an easy target, always in financial trouble. But with all those restrictions in place, how could he have taken enough to matter? It had to be Helen."

"Diabolical."

"But possible? We know she had all that trouble when her son caused that accident. Maybe she was desperate?" Tessa suggested.

"Let's ask her." Mark picked up his phone.

"Wait, what are you doing?" Tessa grabbed his hand to stop him. "You can't just call her and ask her if she's been stealing from the family all this time."

"Can't I?" Mark put the phone back down as he looked into her eyes. "We have all the proof that we need. Tessa, if she really is the thief, and Lisbeth found out about it, that would give her plenty of reason to want to kill her. And maybe she kidnapped Drake because she's still desperate for money?"

"You're right." Tessa pursed her lips as she nodded. "Make the call. It would be better to do it in person, but there's no time to waste. If she has Drake somewhere, we need to find him as soon as possible."

Mark called Helen's cell phone, put the call on speaker, and waited as it rang.

"Hello? Mark?"

"Helen, Tessa's here with me, and we have a couple of questions for you." Mark kept his voice even.

"What questions?" Helen asked.

"When did you make the changes to Stuart Woodcrest's will so you could steal from the family?" Mark demanded.

Tessa held her breath, she knew from years on the force that sometimes you had to be as up front as possible to get the truth out of some people, but it was risky.

"What are you talking about?" Helen's voice rose slightly.

"You know exactly what I'm talking about, so don't bother denying it." Mark's tone hardened further. "You added that list of rules to the will because you knew it would limit how much your clients could withdraw. That gave you plenty of time to drain the account. It was your personal slush fund, ready to use whenever you wanted."

Tessa spoke up. "And whenever a discrepancy came up, you could easily blame Richard. He was in so far over his head, he wasn't keeping track of what he was spending or when he withdrew money from you. But then Lisbeth stepped in. She shut Richard down, and in doing so, she shut you down, too. Without him, you lost your cover. You were out of options. That's when you got desperate, isn't it? You killed Lisbeth and kidnapped Drake, so you'd get a lump sum right away and still have control over the account."

"No! No, you've got it all wrong," Helen gasped.

"Please, you have to believe me, I didn't hurt anyone."

"But you did steal, didn't you?" Tessa leaned closer to the phone. "You haven't denied that."

"Yes, I stole," Helen groaned. "But I didn't hurt Lisbeth. She'd figured out what I'd been doing and she confronted me about it. I begged her not to have me arrested, to give me some time to put the money back. She agreed."

"How did you get the ransom money?" Mark asked.

"I managed to pull it together from other clients' accounts. I couldn't let Drake get hurt." Helen's voice shook. "I didn't kill Lisbeth, I promise. I know what I did is awful, but I never meant to do any harm. It started out with me just taking a few hundred here and there from different accounts. I was desperate for the money. Shortly before Stuart died, my son caused a car accident and people got hurt. The damages were more than I could afford. So, when Stuart died I saw an opportunity and I adjusted his will. I always intended to pay it back, but I was desperate. I had to cover medical bills, repairs, and the legal costs to keep my son out of jail. I thought I could pay it back before anyone noticed, but then the demands just kept coming.

Lawyers and settlements. It snowballed so fast. I never meant for it to get this far, but I didn't know what else to do."

"Well, it did." Tessa sighed. "Even if we believe you, Helen, you're going to have to turn yourself in for stealing from your clients. You realize that, don't you?"

"I do. But right now, that's not what I'm most worried about. Right now, I want to make sure that Drake gets home safe," Helen said.

"If you really felt that way, you would have told Detective Graham, or at the very least, us, about all of this, from the beginning." Tessa clucked her tongue. "You've made a real mess for yourself, and the only way you're going to improve it in any way is if you help us figure out who killed Lisbeth and took Drake."

"If I knew that I would have said something." Helen sighed. "I don't know. I just don't."

"Maybe you don't know, but you do have someone you suspect, don't you?" Tessa pressed as she'd detected the waver in Helen's voice.

CHAPTER 22

*C*assie walked with Sebastian into their home, and she explained what they'd discovered, while Sebastian brewed some tea.

"Here, you sit, and I'll do all the internet searches for you." Sebastian grinned as he set a cup of tea down beside her, along with some of Tessa's homemade chocolate chip cookies. "Just consider me your personal assistant."

"Thank you. I think I could get used to this." Cassie took a sip of her tea as she thought of how different Sebastian was to her first husband. "I want to find out where the money Lisbeth gave to Richard came from. If she needed to give it back, that might be the key. We know Lisbeth borrowed from Gordon, but what if she also borrowed from the same person who lent Richard money? Maybe Gordon's loan wasn't enough, and she was determined to fund the project. But then she gave the money to Richard temporarily because he was desperate."

"And if she borrowed from Richard's lender, they might have been pressuring her to pay up." Sebastian picked up a cookie.

"Or maybe Richard's lender killed Lisbeth because he didn't pay."

"That's possible. Maybe if Richard had multiple loans out and only paid some of them back that might have been enough to make someone lose their temper about not getting their money back. But to kill her?" Sebastian furrowed his brow. "That's a huge consequence."

"True." Cassie had a bite of a cookie. "And the way she was killed in the barn didn't make it look like it was planned. Do you know much about Frank?"

"A bit. He does odd jobs here and there. Friendly enough."

"And what about Gordon?"

"I asked around about him. He bought that property years ago. It used to be an old ranch, and he built that huge house. A friend told me his father offered to work on the build, but Gordon refused and only hired large, out-of-town builders. Rumors say he bribed officials to overlook his underhanded methods. As you know, the historical society's always been strict. I'm surprised he got away with it."

"So, he's used to throwing his money around to get what he wants." Cassie leaned her head back against the couch. "He's a man that doesn't get told no."

"Or, if he does, he doesn't accept it, and uses his money and influence to change the answer." Sebastian glanced up from the computer.

"Maybe. But that doesn't make him a murderer. It still doesn't add up that he would kill Lisbeth. Even if for some reason he wanted the money back he'd invested with her, killing her wouldn't have gotten that. But there were quite a few calls between them."

"We know that she wanted money. Maybe those calls were about asking him for more money?" Sebastian raised his eyebrows. "She could have been hoping he would help her out."

"Possibly, but she was still looking for the money the night before, when she argued with Richard."

"I also heard some rumors that Gordon was

accused of fraud before. But I have no idea if they're true."

"Well, that still doesn't make him a murderer. Unless—" Cassie abruptly sat up and snapped her fingers. "Unless Lisbeth found out about the accusations, or had proof they were true. That would explain why she wanted to pay him back so quickly." She jumped to her feet. "If Lisbeth realized Gordon had loaned her dirty money, she'd want to cut ties immediately. She wouldn't want him involved in the riding school at all. She'd do anything to keep him out of her business."

"That makes sense. And maybe she confronted him about it? That might be why he killed her."

"I don't know. I don't think he would take it that far. He's survived all this time by greasing the wheels and dodging the law. Unless she had some kind of irrefutable proof of his crimes, he had no reason to kill her. But I'm not sure. I want to speak to him again. I want to find out why he didn't mention to the police that Danny was back in town." Cassie chewed on her bottom lip. "And I still want to see if we're missing more of a connection between him and Lisbeth."

"A relationship?"

"Maybe. Only one way to find out." Cassie

grabbed her phone. "I'll see if Tessa wants to meet me over there. We were planning on asking him about Danny, anyway."

"Cassie, it's getting late." Sebastian gestured to the cozy setup on the couch. "Stay, relax, I'll make us some dinner, and you can talk to him tomorrow."

"I'm sorry, I know you're trying to take care of me, but I can't relax until I know who's behind this and Drake's back home."

"Okay, why don't you and Tessa go and talk to Gordon, then come back here for a quick dinner? I'll make us some pasta and meatballs. One of Tessa's favorites. You can't get this solved on an empty stomach."

"Thank you." Cassie kissed him. "You really are amazing."

CHAPTER 23

Tessa focused on Mark's phone as she listened to every word that Helen said.

"I don't know who's responsible for all of this. Kim and Jill had been pressuring me with a lawsuit to appeal the will, but then they suddenly dropped it." Helen hesitated for a moment. "When Lisbeth was found dead, I immediately thought of them. They were furious about being excluded from the ranch, and they discovered the money was missing. If they suspected it was somehow missing because of Lisbeth and her brothers, I could see them being angry enough to do this."

"Is there anything else that you're holding back, Helen?" Tessa tried to keep her tone amicable. "Now's the time to tell the truth."

"There actually is something but it's probably nothing," Helen said.

"What is it?" Tessa asked.

"The last time I had a meeting with Lisbeth—" Helen paused for a moment. "It was a few days ago. When I arrived at the ranch she was talking to Dr. Jacobs, their vet. They saw me and they stopped talking and he hurried off. I felt as if they were hiding something and she seemed upset. When I asked if everything was okay, she just brushed me off."

"So, you have no idea what it was about?" Tessa asked.

"No," Helen replied.

"Anything else?" Mark's voice had an edge to it.

"There's nothing else. I promise." Helen ended the call.

"I can't believe she did that to her clients." Mark looked at Tessa. "I don't do everything aboveboard, you know that, but I would never betray my clients. Whatever I do is to help them."

"I know." Tessa started to say more, but a text on her phone caught her attention. She checked it, then looked up at Mark. "I'm sorry, it's Cassie. She wants to speak to Gordon again, now. And I want to speak to Dr. Jacobs to see if I can find out what his conversation that Helen mentioned was about." She leaned close and placed a light kiss on his cheek. "Thank you for your help."

"Anytime." Mark reached for her hand as she turned away. "Tessa, be careful."

"I will be." Tessa squeezed his hand before she headed for the door. "I promise." She sent a quick text to Cassie offering to pick her up, then rushed to her jeep and headed toward Cassie's house.

Cassie hurried over to the passenger side of Tessa's jeep as soon as she pulled up.

Tessa looked at her as she opened the door. "So, what did you find out?"

"Apparently, there are rumors that there are accusations of fraud against Gordon. I want to ask him about them and try and figure out why he invested money in the business in the first place. I still think there might be more to his relationship with Lisbeth than he's revealed."

"Okay, let's see what we can find out. Hopefully, he's feeling better and can give us some answers." Tessa drove in the direction of Gordon's house. "I do have some things to tell you about Helen." She filled her in on what she and Mark had discovered.

"Wow, she really is a piece of work." Cassie shook her head. "There's no excuse for that."

"I know. She crossed a line, and there's no coming back from that." Tessa parked in front of Gordon's house. "I don't see his car. So, he might not be in." She strode up to the front door.

The door swung open, and a woman who looked a few years younger than Tessa stood in the doorway. Her silver hair was pulled back into a neat bun.

"Joanna." Tessa knew Joanna from when she used to work at the library. "It's good to see you."

"Tessa! And Cassie, too. It's been a while." Joanna smiled as she glanced between them.

"We were hoping to speak with Gordon," Cassie said.

"You've just missed him. He's gone out to a business meeting." Joanna opened the door wider. "Come in."

"Thank you. Are you a friend of his?" Tessa led the way past Joanna into the entrance.

A faint scent caught Cassie's attention immediately. She exchanged a quick glance with Tessa before her eyes landed on the flickering candle sitting on a small coffee table in the living room. The flowery aroma was unmistakable. It was the same as the one in Helen's office.

"No, I'm his housekeeper. After leaving the

library, I picked up a few jobs here and there for extra cash." Joanna turned toward them. "I come by regularly to help keep things in order."

"That candle smells familiar." Cassie tried to sound casual. "Do you know where it's from?"

"Drake gave it to Gordon. He said it was a new business venture he wanted him to invest in. He always has a new business venture to pitch to Gordon." Joanna pursed her lips. "Gordon never bothers with candles, so I light it sometimes. It makes the place feel warmer."

Before Cassie could ask anything else, Tessa chimed in. "Did you know Lisbeth and her brothers well?"

"Gordon's mentioned them a few times, and I've seen them around over the years, but I don't know them well. And I've met Chase briefly, because he's been on the property, once when Lisbeth's horse got loose, because of a break in their fence. I actually saw him by the creek while I was walking here, but he seemed deep in conversation with Kim, and I didn't want to interrupt."

"Kim? Lisbeth's cousin?" Cassie asked.

"Yes." Joanna clasped her hands together. "I think he might be dating her."

"I don't think so. Chase is dating someone else."

As Cassie said the words, a flicker of doubt entered her mind.

"Oh, I must have read too much into it. I always let my imagination run away with me." Joanna waved her hand through the air. "Anyway, can I offer you something to drink? Tea, coffee?"

"That's very kind of you, but we won't keep you. Just let Gordon know we stopped by, please." Tessa smiled.

"Sure. I'll be sure to pass on the message." Joanna opened the door for them.

As Cassie and Tessa stepped outside, the cool breeze was a sharp contrast to the warm, candle-scented room they'd just left. Cassie turned to Tessa.

"That candle," Cassie murmured. "It's the same scent Helen was burning."

"I also recognized it. Drake probably wanted Helen to invest in the company as well. What about what Joanna said about Chase and Kim?"

"Chase mentioned he likes Kim. Maybe they did this together?" Cassie started down the driveway.

"Possibly." Tessa's phone beeped with a text. She read it over, then looked at Cassie. "It's from Ollie. He went to talk to Danny at his father's house, and his brother said he's taken off."

"Oh, that does make him look very suspicious. If

he has Drake somewhere, maybe he's hiding out there?"

"That's what I was thinking. Ollie's going to try and find him." Tessa walked back toward the jeep. "I would still like to stop by and check on Dr. Jacobs after?" Tessa explained that Helen had mentioned a secretive conversation between him and Lisbeth. "And I still want to take him that cherry pie. His arm must be making things difficult."

"Good idea," Cassie agreed.

After picking up the pie from Tessa's, they drove past the clinic to find it closed.

"We can try his house?" Tessa suggested.

"Okay," Cassie said.

Tessa drove the few minutes to his home. As they pulled up outside the three-bedroom house, Cassie noticed that it needed a fresh coat of paint, and the yard needed mowing.

"I know Lynn was staying here with Dr. Jacobs until she finds a place. But I'm not sure if she has, yet." Tessa noticed that there were no cars in the driveway, though she knew they could be in the garage.

Cassie knocked on the front door. When there was no response, she rang the doorbell and still got nothing. She paused, sniffing the air.

"I can smell something. Baking. Cinnamon and spices. Apple pie, maybe? Or muffins." The aroma made Cassie's stomach rumble. "It smells delicious."

"Maybe we didn't need to bring the pie after all."

"No one would ever turn down your baking." Cassie smiled.

Tessa looked at her phone as it beeped. "I just got a text from Lynn. She saw us on the doorbell camera. Dr. Jacobs is having dinner at a friend's house and Lynn's over an hour away."

"It's getting late. We'll have to drop it off tomorrow."

"I'll let her know." Tessa typed out the text, then looked up at Cassie.

"Sebastian just texted that dinner's ready. He made us spaghetti and meatballs. Let's eat, and then we can sort out what to do next."

"Good idea. That's so nice of him." Tessa opened the passenger door.

CHAPTER 24

"Thank you so much for dinner. Delicious as always." Tessa smiled at Sebastian before she headed toward the door. They'd spent most of the time discussing what they'd learned but hadn't come up with anything new, and Tessa was eager to get to the crime scene. She hoped it would hold some answers.

"We won't be long." Cassie gave Sebastian a quick kiss.

"Okay, be careful. It's getting late." Sebastian watched Cassie and Tessa walk toward the jeep.

Tessa started the engine and headed in the direction of the ranch.

"I keep feeling like we're overlooking something." Cassie read over her notes, then looked over at Tessa. "But I can't place what it is. We know that the killer's likely very familiar with the family and the ranch, and we know that money might have been involved in some way. But honestly, I'm almost back to believing that Richard and Drake staged this whole thing."

"It's still a possibility." Tessa turned down the driveway of the ranch. "Now that we know Helen was stealing from the family account and that Lisbeth found out about it, it's also more likely that she could have killed her. The deeper we dig, the more suspicious everyone surrounding Lisbeth becomes. And then, of course, there's Danny and his family. I also want to try to talk to Chase again while we're out there. Maybe there really is more to his relationship with Kim."

"Maybe Chase would kidnap Drake to get the ransom money. But I really don't see Chase as a murderer"—Cassie peered through the windshield as Tessa parked a few feet away from the barn—"especially not Lisbeth. He seemed so devastated, and she was the only one who gave him a chance. I could be wrong, of course. But I mean what would Chase gain from it? Richard's likely to fire him now that Lisbeth's dead." She stepped down out of the jeep.

Tessa joined her at the entrance of the barn. "Let me see if I can get inside." She tried the door, but it didn't open. "It has some kind of digital lock on it." She studied the lock. "If this door was locked when Lisbeth was killed, how did the killer get in?"

"That's a good question. They must have known the code."

"Or." Tessa narrowed her eyes.

"Or?"

"Or, she let the killer in. Which means she most likely trusted them," Tessa suggested.

Cassie pulled out her phone. "Maybe we can get the code from Richard or Chase." She froze at the sound of footsteps not far from her. Darkness had layered thick across the ranch, and though she could hear the footsteps, she could only barely make out a figure approaching.

"Who's there?" Tessa went into alert mode as the figure slowly walked toward them. She activated the flashlight on her phone and pointed it at the silhouette. What the light revealed left her breathless. "Drake?"

Cassie stared at the man who approached her. Aside from his dirt-streaked face and mussed hair he looked fine.

Cassie heard Tessa gasp beside her, but she

couldn't tear her eyes away from the man who stared back at her just as incredulously.

"Who are you? Where's my sister? Where's Richard?" Drake asked.

"Drake!" Without thinking, Cassie instinctively threw her arms around his neck and hugged him. "Are you okay?"

"I'm fine." Drake attempted to free himself of her grasp. "I don't understand. Who are you?"

"I'm Cassie. I've been looking for you." Cassie blushed as she took a step back from him and glanced at Tessa. "We all have. I'm just so glad to see that you're okay."

Cassie looked him over again, and aside from his messy appearance he looked unharmed.

"I've texted Ollie, and called for an ambulance." Tessa rushed over to them. "Drake, how did you get free?"

"I didn't." Drake stared at Tessa, bewildered. "I mean, I did, but only because the door was unlocked. I tried that door a thousand times while I was locked in there, and it was always locked. But just now I tried it again and it opened. So, I just ran."

"Ran from where, exactly?" Tessa stepped closer to him. "Somewhere nearby?"

"Yes, right here on the property." Drake spun around in a slow circle, then squinted through the thick shadows. "I don't know where, though. It can't be too far. But it's so strange. It was like I was somewhere I'd never been before."

"And do you know who took you?" Tessa asked.

"No idea." Drake blinked a few times. "I didn't see them. When I woke up I was in the horse stall and there was food and water. And they gave me some more, through the feed door, just before I found the door unlocked. So, they never spoke to me."

Flashing ambulance lights lit up the driveway, startling all three of them, just as the front door of the house swung open.

"Who's out there? What's happening?" Richard peered at them from the porch.

"Richard!" Drake gasped as he turned toward his brother.

"Drake?" Richard raced down the steps and threw his arms around him. "Oh, Drake, you're safe!"

Oliver's car screeched to a stop right behind the ambulance. He jumped out and sprinted toward them. "Drake, it's so good to see you." His gaze locked on to the man as Richard finally released him.

As the paramedic began evaluating Drake, Tessa filled Oliver in on what they knew so far.

"You were here on this property? Somewhere that you weren't familiar with?" Oliver narrowed his eyes. "Are you sure about that?"

"Yes, it must be. Unless, it was on Gordon's land. I walked here. I know it sounds a little strange. I can't make sense of it myself." Drake ran his hand through his hair. "If I can just clear my head, I might be able to figure it out."

"Take your time," Cassie said gently, as Richard hovered at Drake's side.

"Drake, you need to understand that the person or people who took you are still on the loose, and anything you can tell me can help me catch them." Oliver searched his eyes.

Tessa still suspected that Drake and Richard could have staged all of this, and she imagined Oliver did as well.

"Do you know where you were being held?" Oliver asked.

"I was in a horse stall. I know I was." Drake looked up at Oliver. "Everything about it looked like a horse stall, but it was much smaller and older than any I've seen on the property before."

"How long have you been walking? From what direction?" Oliver glanced around.

"I don't know. I just walked toward the lights." Drake pointed at the ranch house. "I haven't been walking that long. I'm not sure exactly where I came from. My head's so fuzzy."

"You're probably in shock." The paramedic put away the blood pressure monitor. "Your vitals are good, but it would be best to get you to the hospital for a full evaluation."

"Okay. Lisbeth," Drake whispered his sister's name. "Oh no! No, no!" His voice faltered. "She's gone. I remember that. I remember hearing her shout at someone in the barn when I was starting out on my walk, so I went to see if she was okay, then I saw her on the ground, and then everything went black. Something hit me on the head." He rubbed the back of his head. "Then I woke up in the stall."

"We really should get him to the hospital so he can get checked out properly." The paramedic eased him onto a stretcher.

"I'll go with him." Richard followed the stretcher to the ambulance.

"I should, too. If he says anything more about his abductor, I want to be there to hear it. I'm going to have some officers come out here and search the area." Oliver hopped in the ambulance behind Drake and Richard.

The moment it pulled away, Cassie looked over at Tessa.

"We need to help find that horse stall." Tessa's voice was filled with determination. "The quicker it's found, the better."

CHAPTER 25

"I agree. We need to help find that horse stall, but I'm not sure how we're going to locate it." Cassie glanced around her.

"Maybe we can trace Drake's movements." Tessa pointed her phone's flashlight at the ground. "See? There are some scuff marks in the dirt, and some footprints headed that way." She pointed down a narrow path that led away from the house.

"Let's give it a shot." Cassie followed along behind Tessa. "I left my phone in the jeep. We'll have to share your light." For several minutes they trudged through an overgrown area of the ranch.

"There, see that?" Tessa pointed out some torn vines and a thin snapped branch from a low-hanging tree. "He must have come this way."

"It's so thick." Cassie scanned the area. "Do you really think he made his way through that?"

"I think it just looks thick. And I think this borders Gordon's property." Tessa pulled back the vines until she revealed a wall. "Yes! We found something! Let's go around to the other side. There must be a way in."

"Over here!" Cassie rounded the other side of the clump of vines and trees and found a slightly open door. "This must be it." She tugged the door a little farther open and peered inside. "Tessa, we should let Ollie know right away."

"I just called him," a familiar voice spoke up from just beyond the small horse stall.

"Lynn?" Tessa craned her neck in an attempt to see her.

"I thought you were an hour away?" Cassie narrowed her eyes as Lynn stepped into view.

"I just got back." Lynn brushed a strand of hair from her face.

"How did you find this place?" Cassie asked.

"I was walking around, and I just stumbled upon it." Lynn shrugged. "My grandfather always talks about how big the property is, and I wanted to get a feel for it, since I'm the ranch's vet."

"It's so well-hidden." Tessa brushed away some of the thick vines that had once guarded the door. "Maybe this is where Drake was being held."

The clouds shifted, casting a beam of moonlight across Lynn's face, highlighting the rigid set of her jaw and the emptiness in her eyes. A chill ran down Tessa's spine.

"Cassie, we should make sure Ollie gets out here as fast as he can. Do you have your phone?" Tessa looked over at her and held her gaze for a moment.

"No, I left it in the jeep." Cassie had told her that not long ago. Tessa had a sharp mind. What was she up to?

"We can call from the jeep." Tessa's gaze lingered on Lynn. "We should be heading back."

Cassie turned toward the path leading back to the jeep and suddenly gasped. *Baking? How could I smell fresh baking if no one was home?*

Lynn grabbed Cassie hard by the arm and yanked her close, locking her other arm around her. "Not so fast. We're settling this now."

"What are you doing?" Cassie twisted against her grip. "Let me go!"

"Let her go. Right now!" Tessa charged forward, her voice sharp.

Lynn dragged Cassie sideways, positioning her between herself and Tessa, then shoved them both back through the narrow opening of the horse stall.

"Don't do this, Lynn!" Tessa stumbled and grabbed the wooden divider for balance.

Cassie whipped around, fists raised, just as the heavy stall door slammed shut inches from her face. She heard the scrape of metal against metal, followed by a solid click as something was locked into place.

"Let us out!" Cassie gripped the bars at the top of the stall door and glared at Lynn through them.

"I'm sorry it has to be like this." Lynn's voice faltered. "I knew that things weren't going to plan, and I wasn't going to get the money without being caught. So, I let Drake go. I thought his release would be enough of a distraction to give me time to clean up any evidence here. I knew this had already gone too far. I would never get the money back for my grandfather and extra for security. Then you two came looking and found me here. I misjudged how quickly anyone would find this place. I can't let you turn me in. Do you understand? I can't go to prison."

"You were at your grandfather's house when we knocked on the door." Tessa snapped her fingers.

"That's why we could smell the baking. But you lied about where you were to give yourself an alibi for when Drake was last given food, and the horse stall was unlocked. So, no one would suspect you had anything to do with this."

"Exactly," Lynn said.

"Your grandfather's money? He'd invested in the riding school?" Cassie's mind spun as the pieces began to fall into place.

"Yes, he helped Lisbeth out with some capital from the vet practice, and she just stole it," Lynn snapped.

"Wait." Tessa's tone took on a professional lilt. "Let's be reasonable about this. The truth is you can still get out of all of this. You just have to think it through. Letting Drake go unharmed is something you can use as a bargaining chip with the prosecutor. You just have to get your story straight. I can help you with that. No one really knows what happened between you and Lisbeth. You can come up with whatever makes you look the most innocent. Start by telling me everything, and then from there we can discuss how to change it up to make sure that you only get charged with manslaughter, or maybe you can get away with self-defense."

Tessa sounded so convincing that Cassie almost believed her.

"Yes, let us help you. Just tell us what happened, from the beginning." Cassie glanced over at Tessa and noticed that she'd been trying to subtly dial her phone, but the call wasn't going through.

CHAPTER 26

Lynn stared through the metal bars of the stall door. "Don't bother with your phone. I have a cell-phone jamming device right next to the stall." She let out a short laugh. "I'm not an idiot, you know. And neither is my grandfather. He's just too nice to people." She shook her head. "I came here to help him with his vet practice and the horse-riding school. I gave up my life and invested everything I had into the practice."

"But everything fell apart when you got here because Lisbeth hadn't gotten the school off the ground?" Tessa said.

"Yes. She promised us the contracts to maintain the horses, and I was supposed to slowly take over the practice. It was perfect." Lynn's tone sharpened.

"It made me think that maybe my relationship ending, my life falling apart, wasn't such a bad thing. Maybe I could finally settle down and be happy. My grandfather believed that since Gordon had invested, and Gordon knows what he's doing, it had to be a good deal. But when I got here, I realized something was wrong. Nothing had been set up. Lisbeth hadn't gotten any of it off the ground."

"So, you got suspicious?" Tessa's mind raced as she tried to think of a way out of there.

"Not really. My grandfather trusted her, so I trusted her." Lynn let out a bitter laugh. "But I told him he needed to pull out and get his investment back because she hadn't done anything yet."

"But he refused." Cassie's heart pounded.

"Yes, at first." Lynn nodded. "But I managed to convince him to do something because if he didn't, the practice would go under. Since they set up that new vet clinic in Rombsby, business was suffering, and he eventually agreed. But when he asked for his investment back, Lisbeth said she didn't have it. She needed more time to come up with it. Then nothing happened. She kept delaying him."

"So, you had to do something?" Tessa took a step forward.

"I didn't plan any of it. I came out here early yesterday morning. She was going to introduce me to the horses and give me a tour of the property after she'd fed them. But when I met her in the barn I asked her about the money. She said she couldn't give it back, yet."

"And you needed the money?" Tessa nodded.

"Yes, I had to do something. I didn't have a choice. My grandfather didn't have any paperwork to show he'd given her the money. He's a great person, a wonderful vet, but not the best businessman, to say the least. He's too trusting. I confronted Lisbeth, and she finally admitted that she hadn't even invested the money in getting the riding school set up. She'd given it to Richard." Lynn rolled her eyes. "She'd basically stolen from my grandfather, from me."

"You must have been furious." Tessa tried to sound sympathetic.

"She kept pleading with me to understand and to just give her a little more time. But yes, I was livid. I don't have time. If I didn't get that money back, so we could keep the practice going until we could sort something out, we would lose the business. The practice in Rombsby would have to buy us out, which is what they were hoping to do, so we wouldn't be bankrupted. I would have moved here for nothing. What I'd invested in the vet practice, all my savings, would go to creditors. So, I told her I was taking her most valuable horse, Phantom. I figured I could get some quick cash for him. It might not be as much as we needed, but it would be a start. And she lost it. She said I could take anything but the horse. She screamed at me and lunged toward me. I picked up the hook and swung it at her. I didn't think about it, really. I didn't intend to kill her. When I swung it at her, I think I was just as shocked as she was."

"And you just let her die? You didn't get her help?" Cassie's heart sank.

"Even if I'd wanted to save her, I wouldn't have been able to. And before I could even think about what to do next, Drake came into the barn, and Phantom bolted through the door. I panicked. If Drake saw me in there he would know it was me who killed Lisbeth. So, I hit him over the head before he could see me. But as I stood there, I remembered the story my grandfather had told me about Danny being kidnapped from the Woodcrests' ranch, and how the ransom wasn't paid because he wasn't a family member, and a plan formed..." Lynn's voice trailed off.

"A plan to kidnap Drake? You thought they would hand over the cash because he's family." Tessa tried to keep her talking.

"Yes. I could use him to get it back and more to make sure we were comfortable. I figured once I had the cash, I would release Drake, and no one would know what I'd done, and everything would be fine. They wouldn't even miss it. I mean, look at that ranch. It's worth millions. Part of the money was ours. It was just a little interest for all the trouble Lisbeth put us through. What's so wrong with that?" Lynn glared at them. "But nothing went to plan, and now you found me here."

"Does your grandfather know what you've done?" Tessa asked.

"Of course not." Lynn's voice wavered slightly. "And he's never going to find out. I could never do that to him."

"We can help you get out of this." Cassie tried to sound reassuring.

"Sorry, I'm not taking any chances this time." Lynn turned and disappeared from view.

"Wait! Come back!" Cassie gasped as she pounded on the door. "Please!"

"Save your energy, Cassie. We can get this figured out, but we have to be calm about it." Tessa's voice held a hint of doubt. She began knocking on the walls of the stall. "We just have to find a weak spot."

A couple of minutes later, Cassie heard a muffled male voice outside. It sounded familiar, but she couldn't place it. She felt a wave of relief. At least help was there.

"Hello?" Cassie called out through the bars. "Hello?"

A shadow shifted before a face appeared just beyond the bars. "Hey, there." Chase peered in at them. "What's going on in here?"

CHAPTER 27

"Please help us, Chase!" Cassie curled her fingers around the metal bars again. She wanted to reach through them, but they were too close together. "She's locked us in! It was Lynn! She killed Lisbeth! Please! You have to get us out of here!"

"I'm sorry. I can't do that." Chase backed away.

"What are you doing?" Cassie shrieked. "Let us out!"

"Cassie, he's in on it." Tessa grabbed her hand to pull her away from the door.

Chase appeared just beyond the bars again.

"He's here to finish what Lynn started. That's how Lynn knew about this place." Tessa scowled at Chase.

"Lisbeth took a chance on you." Cassie gazed at him with wide eyes. "How could you betray her like this?"

"She betrayed me first." Chase glared at her. "She was supposed to put me in charge of training all the horses. Between that and the trailer, I was going to be set for the first time in my life. I could finally breathe easy. Then, all of that changed. She told me that she couldn't have a felon working for her when she opened the riding school. She told me that she couldn't have me involved with the school in any way, and that also meant not training the horses. When I told her how unfair that was, she didn't want to hear about it. She kept saying that it was temporary and she would work it out. But I knew she was lying. I knew she'd get rid of me as soon as she'd managed to get someone to replace me. I didn't have a choice."

"But you did have a choice, when you found out that Lynn killed Lisbeth." Tessa shifted closer to Cassie. "You had a chance to do the right thing. Why wouldn't you turn her in after what she did?"

"Turn her in? What good would that do for me." Chase chuckled. "That wasn't an option."

"So, you helped her cover up her crimes?" Cassie asked.

"Yes, I had no choice. When I walked into the stall and saw Lisbeth dead and Drake knocked out, Lynn offered me a deal. She said that if I helped her she would give me some money, and she and her grandfather would help me start my own riding school. I couldn't turn her down. It was a great opportunity. Dr. Jacobs is well-known and respected in the community." Chase ran his hand across his jaw as he looked between the two of them. "And if I didn't help her, she promised me that she would pin the entire murder on me. She knew that I couldn't afford a lawyer."

"How would she pin it on you?" Cassie asked.

"My fingerprints were all over the barn. I could explain them, of course. But she had texts from me as well." Chase shrugged. "I met Lynn at Dr. Jacobs' practice a few days ago. I told her how I probably wouldn't be working at the ranch much longer and why. She said she would let me know if she came across any other possible opportunities for me, and we exchanged numbers. Then I sent her a couple of texts asking if she'd come across any work, because I was sure Lisbeth was going to fire me. So, she could have used the texts as evidence that I had a motive. Mallory gave me an alibi, but it would never stand up under scrutiny."

"You must have been furious with Lisbeth?" Cassie's expression tightened.

"I was, but I never would have killed her. And I couldn't bring her back. It wouldn't have taken much for Lynn to make sure that I would go down for the murder. Instead, all I had to do was keep quiet and help her abduct Drake, and I would get something from it. I'm not going to say it was easy. But it had to be done." Chase shrugged. "We ditched his phone by the barn, so they couldn't trace where we took him, and I helped move him to the horse stall. Again, I had no choice. And now I have to do this. It's nothing personal. It's just that there aren't a lot of options for people like me." He took a step away from the stall door. A second later, the quiet was broken by the unmistakable sloshing of liquid.

Tessa sniffed the air and gasped. "It's gasoline."

Cassie's heart raced at Tessa's words, and she knew she had to do everything she could to get them out of there. She pulled away from Tessa and moved closer to the door. "I think you're wrong. You had a choice, then, just like you have a choice now. You didn't kill anyone, Chase. You can still turn this around. If you do this, there won't be any way out."

"I don't back down that easily." Chase chuckled.

"The only way I go down for anything is if you two are alive to send me to prison."

Cassie watched him warily.

"There are plenty of other suspects to pin all of this on. I was hoping Helen would end up taking the fall. I've never liked her. But if that doesn't work out, I've already set things up to point to Jill and Kim. They trust me. I made sure of that." Chase held up a lighter. "They're the ones who showed me that tree in the middle of the garden. That's how I knew to put the ransom note there. Lynn wrote the note, and I came back and put it on the tree. By that time Lisbeth had been found and the police were there. It'll be easy enough for Lynn and me to steer the police in Kim and Jill's direction. Now, if there were witnesses, yeah, I'd be in deep trouble." He flipped a lighter open, and the flame reflected in his eyes. "But that's not going to be a problem, is it?" He shoved the lighter through the bars above the stall door into a pile of old, dry hay near the front of the stall, just off to the side of the door, then chuckled as he walked away.

Cassie gasped and threw herself against the sturdy wooden door, but it held firm.

The hay inside burned fast. Tessa's heart pounded. She knew it would quickly reach the gasoline he'd spread outside, and once it did the entire stall would be engulfed.

"Cassie, we have to get the fire out!" Tessa began kicking dirt in the direction of the burning hay.

CHAPTER 28

Tessa continued to kick dirt toward the flames that were quickly rising. "Cassie, we need to get as close to the door as we can. If we get trapped in the back there will be no way out."

As Cassie ran over to help her, a loud neigh sounded from outside the stall.

"Tessa, I think there's someone out there!" Cassie skirted the flames toward the door and pounded on it as she coughed, pressing a hand to her throat before she shouted through the bars. "Hello? Is anyone there? Help us, please!"

Another loud neigh sounded, followed by some fierce barks.

"Harry?" Tessa gasped. "It's Harry!"

"Help us! We're in here! Please help!" Cassie yelled, her voice hoarse from the smoke.

"I'm here, Cassie. I'm here!" Sebastian called out as he approached on Phantom. The light from the fire illuminated the thick brush that surrounded the stall. He slid off the horse's back and ran toward the stall with Harry at his side. "I'm here. I'm going to get you both out, hang on!" He fumbled with the lock. "It's padlocked."

"Stand back!" another familiar voice shouted.

"Ollie's out there, too!" Tessa craned her neck in an attempt to see him.

Cassie saw another horse come into view just as Oliver jumped down from its saddle with his gun drawn.

"Tessa, Cassie, shield yourselves!" Oliver warned them a few seconds before firing a bullet at the padlock on the door.

Thick smoke swirled through the horse stall, stinging Cassie's eyes and throat. She pressed a hand over her mouth, but the heat closed in around her, making it harder to breathe. Her heart raced as she tried not to panic.

The door swung open, and two pairs of hands thrust into the stall to help guide them out.

Harry circled them both with low growls and

soft whimpers of concern, and they patted his head reassuringly.

"It's okay, boy." Tessa coughed.

"We should get out of here." Sebastian swung Cassie into his arms, then lifted her up onto Phantom's saddle.

"What are you doing?" Cassie coughed as she tried to clear her lungs. "I can't ride a horse!"

Sebastian jumped up onto the horse behind her and held her tight against him.

Tessa let out a startled shriek as Oliver lifted her onto his horse. Within moments, they were galloping through the thick brush toward the ranch house, with Harry close behind.

Cassie clung on to Sebastian's arm that wrapped around her stomach and held her steady as she bounced and swayed on the horse. Fire truck sirens sounded in the distance.

For the first time, Cassie allowed herself to feel relieved, and safe. She closed her eyes and listened to the sound of the horses' hooves. She could feel Sebastian's heartbeat pounding against her back as he kept a firm hold on her.

When they reached the safety of the ranch, Phantom let out a wild neigh. Cassie stroked his silvery mane. "You did good, Phantom. You did really good."

As Sebastian helped Cassie down off the horse, Tessa looked at Oliver.

"Where did you learn to ride a horse like that?" Tessa asked.

"I spent a few summers with my uncle on his farm and he had horses. He thought it would bring out the man in me to make me train the wildest one." Oliver rolled his eyes. "I still have the scars."

"Well, you did very well just now." Tessa smiled, then blurted out every detail about Lynn and Chase.

"I'll get my officers to pick them up." Oliver nodded to them, then spoke into his radio.

"How did you find us?" Tessa asked.

"When I couldn't locate the two of you, I found Cassie's phone in the jeep. I knew you would try and find where Drake had been held. About that time, Sebastian was hounding me about where you were, so I invited him to help search, and he brought Harry and he sniffed you out. We decided to use the horses to get through the brush and hopefully make better time. Harry stayed on your scent, and then we saw the flames and we found you." Oliver's radio crackled to life. He stepped away as he responded, then turned back to them. "My officers have caught Lynn and Chase."

"Great." Tessa smiled.

"I don't know what possessed you to go off on your own like that, but if it ever happens again, I'll lock you both up." Oliver ran his hands over his face and sighed.

"You and what army?" Tessa snapped.

"You'd have to get past Sebastian first." Cassie smiled as she hugged her husband.

"Oh, don't think I wouldn't help him lock you up." Sebastian's arms tightened around her. "I was so scared. Do you know what could have happened, Cassie?" He pulled back, cupped her cheeks, and looked into her eyes. "I'm never going to lose you, understand?"

Cassie's pulse raced as she saw the mixture of fear and relief in his eyes. She'd been scared herself, but she hadn't thought about it from his point of view, as he rode up to a burning horse stall and heard her screaming for help.

"I'm sorry." Cassie leaned her forehead against his. "It was risky. We should have been more careful."

"She's right." Tessa crouched down to hug Harry. "Sometimes we get a little ahead of ourselves. But the important thing is, we're all safe now." She stood back up and met Oliver's worried gaze. "We're all still here. Thank you for coming to our rescue."

"Of course." Oliver smiled and pulled her into a warm hug.

"At least Lynn and Chase have been caught." Tessa patted his shoulder. "Thanks to you, Ollie."

"Thanks to teamwork." Oliver flashed her a brief smile.

CHAPTER 29

A couple of days later, Cassie spent the morning at Tessa's getting organized for a get-together at the ranch that afternoon. It was Jill and Kim's idea, and although at first Cassie wondered if it was too soon, by the time she left with Sebastian for the event, she understood the wisdom behind it. Chase and Lynn had come onto their family ranch and wounded their family. This was their way of taking it back, and filling it with love and connection once more.

"Kim and Jill's idea of opening a riding school on the Woodcrest ranch is something I think the community is really going to support." Sebastian pulled his truck out onto the street.

"Yes. I think losing Lisbeth has shown her

brothers that family is more important than anything, and they've welcomed their cousins back into their lives. They said they dropped the suit to contest the will because they weren't happy with their lawyer. They were going to look for a new one, but now that things have changed they aren't going to pursue it."

"Gordon has agreed to invest a bit more money in the school, and Kim texted a few of my connections earlier today to see if they would help make it happen. With Dr. Jacobs' help we all agreed to guide the family through whatever hurdles there might be, and find the resources that they need. And, of course, it's something for Dr. Jacobs to concentrate on after what Lynn did." Sebastian turned down the long drive that led to the ranch. "And did you hear, apparently the clinic in Rombsby is going to join with the one here, so Dr. Jacobs can still slowly retire, but he'll be fine financially."

"Oh, that is good news." Cassie glanced over at Sebastian as he parked. "After what Lynn did, he needs all the support he can get."

"Absolutely." Sebastian smiled as he got out of the truck and walked around it to open the door for her. "I hope I get a slice of that cherry pie. It smelled so delicious when Tessa was baking it this morning."

"Don't worry, I made one just for you. Well, Tessa did help me a bit." Cassie blushed as she stepped out of the truck. "It might not be as tasty as Tessa's, but I think I did a good job."

"I'm sure you did. I can't wait to try a slice." Sebastian smiled.

Cassie grabbed Sebastian's hand and glanced around the ranch.

Already, a large crowd had formed around the main riding arena of the ranch, where several horses, including Phantom, were giving short rides to the community. In another smaller enclosure, Gerry and Billy chased each other and several small children, while Harry did his best to keep the squealing children safe. Cassie laughed at the sight, then looked back at the horses. She leaned against the railing and watched Phantom walk around the arena.

"Cassie!" Tessa walked over, then tipped her head toward the man beside her. "Mark insisted on driving me here. He said something about the precious cargo needing a delicate touch behind the wheel." She rolled her eyes.

"Well, you are precious cargo, Tessa." Cassie smiled.

"He was talking about the pies." Tessa laughed.

"Was I?" Mark kissed the top of her head.

"Mark!" Tessa scowled.

"Again?" Mark grinned as he leaned close just before she ducked out of the way.

As Cassie watched the two walk off, playfully arguing, she couldn't help but laugh. She glanced over at Sebastian and smiled at the sight of him in his cowboy hat. Despite owning a farm and his Southern drawl, she'd never thought of him as a cowboy before. At least, not until he took her for a ride on Phantom.

"I know I was scared, but I was really impressed with how you handled the horse when you saved us, Sebastian. I feel like there's a whole side of you I didn't even know about." Cassie reached up and tugged at the brim of his hat. "Thanks for not letting me fall off."

"You did great." Sebastian leaned closer to her. "In fact, I think you're a natural."

"A natural?" Cassie laughed. "That was the first time I'd ever been on a horse. I have no idea how to ride one."

"Well, now's the perfect time to change that." Sebastian looked at Jill who walked over with Phantom. He held his hand out, and Jill passed him the reins, then he offered Cassie his other hand. He led her into the ring, then gave Phantom a few strokes on the neck before he looked back at Cassie. "Let's get you up there."

"Up there?" Cassie glanced at the saddle, then back at him. "I don't know."

"I do." Sebastian flashed her a confident smile before lifting her gently by the waist. "I know you can do absolutely anything you put your mind to."

He eased her onto the saddle, keeping hold of the reins.

"I'll be right here to catch you." Sebastian patted her knee. "You've got this. I promise."

Cassie felt a sudden sense of peace as she gazed down into his eyes and saw the certainty there. She'd led an eventful life, going from having little, to having far more than she would ever need, before her husband's unexpected death had forced her to start over. But never had she felt as lucky as she did in that moment, adored by a man who she loved just as deeply, and surrounded by friends who had become family.

The End

❉❉❉

Thank you for reading *Kidnapped in Little Leaf Creek*. I loved writing it and I hope you enjoyed reading it. Ready for more of Cassie and Tessa's sleuthing adventures? The next book in the series is *Heist in Little Leaf Creek.* If you'd like to receive an email when I have a new release, please join my cozy mystery newsletter at www.cindybellbooks.com.

TESSA'S LATTICE CHERRY PIE RECIPE

Ingredients:

Pie Crust

2 1/2 cups all-purpose flour, plus more for dusting
1/2 teaspoon salt
2 tablespoons granulated sugar
1 cup (8 ounces) very cold unsalted butter, cut into cubes
4 to 8 tablespoons ice cold water

Filling

5 cups fresh or frozen cherries, pitted and sliced into a mixture of halves and quarters. (Frozen pitted

TESSA'S LATTICE CHERRY PIE RECIPE

cherries do not need to be thawed first before slicing.)

1/4 cup cornstarch

3/4 cup granulated sugar

1 tablespoon lemon juice

1 teaspoon vanilla extract

1 teaspoon almond extract

1/4 teaspoon salt

1 tablespoon cold unsalted butter, cut into small cubes

For the egg wash: 1 large egg and 1 tablespoon milk

Preparation:

For the pie crust, mix the flour, salt, and sugar in a bowl.

Cut in the cold cubed butter with a pastry cutter or rub it in with your fingertips, until the mixture resembles fine breadcrumbs.

Gradually add the water until the dough can be formed into a ball. Add just enough water for the dough to hold together but not feel sticky.

TESSA'S LATTICE CHERRY PIE RECIPE

The pastry can also be made in a food processor.

Divide the prepared pastry into two portions and shape them into disks. One portion should be about two thirds of the dough which is used for the bottom and sides of the pie. The other third is for the lattice top.

Wrap the dough with plastic wrap and refrigerate for at least an hour.

To make the filling, place the cherries, cornstarch, sugar, lemon juice, vanilla extract, almond extract, and salt, in a bowl, and stir together to coat the cherries.

Remove the cooled dough from the fridge.

If the pastry is too firm to roll, leave it at room temperature for 5 to 10 minutes.

Preheat the oven to 400 degrees Fahrenheit.

On a lightly floured surface, roll out the larger portion of the dough and use it to line the bottom and sides of a 9-inch pie dish. Trim the sides.

TESSA'S LATTICE CHERRY PIE RECIPE

Spoon in the cherry mixture, but don't add the excess juice because it will make the pastry soggy.

Dot the cubes of butter over the filling.

To make the lattice top, roll out the other portion of the pastry to fit the top of the pie. Cut into 1-inch strips.

Take the strips of pastry and carefully weave them to form a lattice on the top of the pie. Crimp the edges.

Lightly beat the egg and milk together and brush over the pastry using a pastry brush.

Place the pie in the preheated oven and bake for about 30 to 40 minutes, until the pastry is golden and the filling is bubbling. If the edges brown too quickly, cover them with foil to prevent burning.

Let the pie cool at room temperature for about 2 to 3 hours before cutting.

Enjoy!!

ABOUT THE AUTHOR

Cindy Bell is a USA Today and Wall Street Journal Bestselling Author. She is the author of over one hundred books in thirteen series. Her cozies are set in small towns, with lovable animals, quirky characters, delicious food and a touch of romance. She loves writing twisty cozy mysteries that keep readers guessing until the end.

When she is not reading or writing, she loves baking (and eating) sweet treats or walking along the beach with Rufus, her energetic Cocker Spaniel, thinking of the next adventure her characters can embark on.

If you'd like to receive an email when she has a new release, please join her cozy mystery newsletter at https://www.cindybellbooks.com.

ALSO BY CINDY BELL

LTTLE LEAF CREEK COZY MYSTERIES

[Little Leaf Creek Cozy Mystery Series 10 Book Box Set (Books 1-10)](#)

[Little Leaf Creek Cozy Mystery Series 10 Book Box Set (Books 11-20)](#)

[Little Leaf Creek Cozy Mystery Series Box Set Vol 1 (Books 1-3)](#)

[Little Leaf Creek Cozy Mystery Series Box Set Vol 2 (Books 3-6)](#)

[Little Leaf Creek Cozy Mystery Series Box Set Vol 3 (Books 7-9)](#)

[Little Leaf Creek Cozy Mystery Series Box Set Vol 4 (Books 10-12)](#)

[Little Leaf Creek Cozy Mystery Series Box Set Vol 5 (Books 13-15)](#)

[Chaos in Little Leaf Creek](#)

[Peril in Little Leaf Creek](#)

[Conflict in Little Leaf Creek](#)

[Action in Little Leaf Creek](#)

[Vengeance in Little Leaf Creek](#)

- [Greed in Little Leaf Creek](#)
- [Surprises in Little Leaf Creek](#)
- [Missing in Little Leaf Creek](#)
- [Haunted in Little Leaf Creek](#)
- [Trouble in Little Leaf Creek](#)
- [Mayhem In Little Leaf Creek](#)
- [Cracked in Little Leaf Creek](#)
- [Stung in Little Leaf Creek](#)
- [Scandal In Little Leaf Creek](#)
- [Dead in Little Leaf Creek](#)
- [Scared in Little Leaf Creek](#)
- [Felled in Little Leaf Creek](#)
- [Deceit in Little Leaf Creek](#)
- [Secrets in Little Leaf Creek](#)
- [Poisoned in Little Leaf Creek](#)
- [Silenced in Little Leaf Creek](#)
- [Last Dance in Little Leaf Creek](#)
- [Broken in Little Leaf Creek](#)
- [Skeletons in Little Leaf Creek](#)
- [Trailed in Little Leaf Creek](#)
- [Kidnapped in Little Leaf Creek](#)
- [Heist in Little Leaf Creek](#)

LAKESIDE COTTAGE COZY MYSTERIES

A Murky Murder

A Perilous Package

A Fatal Focus

A Deadly Dunk

CHOCOLATE CENTERED COZY MYSTERIES

Chocolate Centered Cozy Mystery 10 Book Box Set (Books 1 - 10)

Chocolate Centered Cozy Mystery Series Box Set (Books 1 - 4)

Chocolate Centered Cozy Mystery Series Box Set (Books 5 - 8)

Chocolate Centered Cozy Mystery Series Box Set (Books 9 - 12)

Chocolate Centered Cozy Mystery Series Box Set (Books 13 - 16)

The Sweet Smell of Murder

A Deadly Delicious Delivery

A Bitter Sweet Murder

A Treacherous Tasty Trail

Pastry and Peril

Trouble and Treats

Fudge Films and Felonies

Custom-Made Murder

Skydiving, Soufflés and Sabotage

Christmas Chocolates and Crimes

Hot Chocolate and Homicide

Chocolate Caramels and Conmen

Picnics, Pies and Lies

Devils Food Cake and Drama

Cinnamon and a Corpse

Cherries, Berries and a Body

Christmas Cookies and Criminals

Grapes, Ganache & Guilt

Yule Logs & Murder

Mocha, Marriage and Murder

Holiday Fudge and Homicide

Chocolate Mousse and Murder

Salted Caramels, Shows, and Suspects

Peppermint Bark and Peril

Birthday Cake and Betrayal

LITTLE LEAF CREEK COZY MYSTERIES

Little Leaf Creek Cozy Mystery Series 10 Book Box Set (Books 1-10)

Little Leaf Creek Cozy Mystery Series 10 Book Box Set (Books 11-20)

Little Leaf Creek Cozy Mystery Series Box Set Vol 1 (Books 1-3)

Little Leaf Creek Cozy Mystery Series Box Set Vol 2 (Books 3-6)

Little Leaf Creek Cozy Mystery Series Box Set Vol 3 (Books 7-9)

Little Leaf Creek Cozy Mystery Series Box Set Vol 4 (Books 10-12)

Little Leaf Creek Cozy Mystery Series Box Set Vol 5 (Books 13-15)

Chaos in Little Leaf Creek

Peril in Little Leaf Creek

Conflict in Little Leaf Creek

Action in Little Leaf Creek

Vengeance in Little Leaf Creek

Greed in Little Leaf Creek

Surprises in Little Leaf Creek

Missing in Little Leaf Creek

Haunted in Little Leaf Creek

Trouble in Little Leaf Creek

Mayhem In Little Leaf Creek

Cracked in Little Leaf Creek

Stung in Little Leaf Creek

Scandal In Little Leaf Creek

Dead in Little Leaf Creek

Scared in Little Leaf Creek

Felled in Little Leaf Creek

Deceit in Little Leaf Creek

Secrets in Little Leaf Creek

Poisoned in Little Leaf Creek

Silenced in Little Leaf Creek

Last Dance in Little Leaf Creek

Broken in Little Leaf Creek

Skeletons in Little Leaf Creek

Trailed in Little Leaf Creek

Kidnapped in Little Leaf Creek

DUNE HOUSE COZY MYSTERIES

Dune House Cozy Mystery Series 10 Book Box Set (Books 1 - 10)

Dune House Cozy Mystery Series 10 Book Box Set 2 (Books 11 - 20)

Dune House Cozy Mystery Series Boxed Set 1 (Books 1 - 4)

Dune House Cozy Mystery Series Boxed Set 2 (Books 5 - 8)

Dune House Cozy Mystery Series Boxed Set 3 (Books 9 - 12)

Dune House Cozy Mystery Series Boxed Set 4 (Books 13 - 16)

Seaside Secrets

Boats and Bad Guys

Treasured History

Hidden Hideaways

Dodgy Dealings

Suspects and Surprises

Ruffled Feathers

A Fishy Discovery

Danger in the Depths

Celebrities and Chaos

Pups, Pilots and Peril

Tides, Trails and Trouble

Racing and Robberies

Athletes and Alibis

Manuscripts and Deadly Motives

Pelicans, Pier and Poison

Sand, Sea and a Skeleton

Pianos and Prison

Relaxation, Reunions and Revenge

A Tangled Murder

Fame, Food and Murder

Beaches and Betrayal

Fatal Festivities

Sunsets, Smoke and Suspicion

Hobbies and Homicide

Anchors and Abduction

Friends, Family and Fugitives

Palm Trees and Protests

Road Trip, Risk and Revenge

Fruit Smoothies and Felonies

Sunshine, Scents, and Suspects

Docks, Discoveries, and Danger

SAGE GARDENS COZY MYSTERIES

Sage Gardens Cozy Mystery 10 Book Box Set (Books 1 - 10)

[Sage Gardens Cozy Mystery Series Box Set Volume 1 (Books 1 - 4)](#)

[Sage Gardens Cozy Mystery Series Box Set Volume 2 (Books 5 - 8)](#)

[Birthdays Can Be Deadly](#)

[Money Can Be Deadly](#)

[Trust Can Be Deadly](#)

[Ties Can Be Deadly](#)

[Rocks Can Be Deadly](#)

[Jewelry Can Be Deadly](#)

[Numbers Can Be Deadly](#)

[Memories Can Be Deadly](#)

[Paintings Can Be Deadly](#)

[Snow Can Be Deadly](#)

[Tea Can Be Deadly](#)

[Greed Can Be Deadly](#)

[Clutter Can Be Deadly](#)

[Cruises Can Be Deadly](#)

[Puzzles Can Be Deadly](#)

[Concerts Can Be Deadly](#)

MADDIE MILLS COZY MYSTERIES

Maddie Mills Cozy Mysteries Books 1 - 3

Slain at the Sea

Homicide at the Harbor

Corpse at the Christmas Cookie Exchange

Lifeless at the Lighthouse

Halloween at the Haunted House

DONUT TRUCK COZY MYSTERIES

Deadly Deals and Donuts

Fatal Festive Donuts

Bunny Donuts and a Body

Strawberry Donuts and Scandal

Frosted Donuts and Fatal Falls

Donut Holes and Homicide

WAGGING TAIL COZY MYSTERIES

Wagging Tail Cozy Mystery Box Set Volume 1 (Books 1 - 3)

Murder at Pawprint Creek (prequel)

Murder at Pooch Park

Murder at the Pet Boutique

A Merry Murder at St. Bernard Cabins

Murder at the Dog Training Academy

Murder at Corgi Country Club

A Merry Murder on Ruff Road

Murder at Poodle Place

Murder at Hound Hill

Murder at Rover Meadows

Murder at the Pet Expo

Murder on Woof Way

Murder at Beagle Bay

NUTS ABOUT NUTS COZY MYSTERIES

A Tough Case to Crack

A Seed of Doubt

Roasted Peanuts and Peril

Chestnuts, Camping and Culprits

BEKKI THE BEAUTICIAN COZY MYSTERIES

Hairspray and Homicide

A Dyed Blonde and a Dead Body

Mascara and Murder

Pageant and Poison

Conditioner and a Corpse

Mistletoe, Makeup and Murder

Hairpin, Hair Dryer and Homicide

Blush, a Bride and a Body

Shampoo and a Stiff

Cosmetics, a Cruise and a Killer

Lipstick, a Long Iron and Lifeless

Camping, Concealer and Criminals

Treated and Dyed

A Wrinkle-Free Murder

A MACARON PATISSERIE COZY MYSTERY

Sifting for Suspects

Recipes and Revenge

Mansions, Macarons and Murder

HEAVENLY HIGHLAND INN COZY MYSTERIES

Murdering the Roses

Dead in the Daisies

Killing the Carnations

Drowning the Daffodils

Suffocating the Sunflowers

Books, Bullets and Blooms

A Deadly Serious Gardening Contest

A Bridal Bouquet and a Body

Digging for Dirt

WENDY THE WEDDING PLANNER COZY MYSTERIES

Matrimony, Money and Murder

Chefs, Ceremonies and Crimes

Knives and Nuptials

Mice, Marriage and Murder

Made in United States
Troutdale, OR
03/19/2025